WHERE DREAMS COME TRUE

The Daily Cruise Letter/The Daily Cruise News

Come up to the Helios deck and meet our golf pro, Eric Lashman. Eric spent eight seasons on the pro tour and won two majors, so the staff of *Alexandra's Dream* is thrilled to have him on board.

Don't worry if you're not a golfer. All passengers are entitled to a free lesson with Eric on our state-of-the-art driving range and putting green. And if you're a seasoned golfer, be sure to sign up for shore excursions with Eric to some of the Mediterranean's finest courses. You can swing your clubs in Rome and Naples, with a special visit to Le Maquis on the fascinating island of Corsica.

For golfers and nongolfers alike, plan to attend Father Patrick Connelly's lecture on Etruscan art and architecture in the library this morning. *Alexandra's Dream* is delighted to have an expert in classical antiquities this season. Your visits to the museums in Naples and Rome will be all the more rewarding after one of Father Pat's talks.

So relax and enjoy. We're here to make your Mediterranean days and nights the most memorable of your life.

MARISA CARROLL

is the pen name of authors Carol Wagner and Marian Franz. The team has been writing bestselling books for twenty-five years. During that time they have published over forty titles, most for the Harlequin Superromance line, and are the recipients of several industry awards, including a Lifetime Achievement award from *Romantic Times BOOKreviews* and a RITA® Award nomination from Romance Writers of America. The sisters live near each other in rural northwestern Ohio, surrounded by children, grandchildren, brothers, sisters, aunts, uncles, cousins and old and dear friends.

Mediterranean NIGHTS™

Marisa Carroll

BREAKING ALL THE RULES

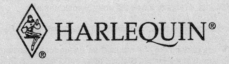

HARLEQUIN®

TORONTO • NEW YORK • LONDON
AMSTERDAM • PARIS • SYDNEY • HAMBURG
STOCKHOLM • ATHENS • TOKYO • MILAN • MADRID
PRAGUE • WARSAW • BUDAPEST • AUCKLAND

ISBN-13: 978-0-373-38963-6
ISBN-10:   0-373-38963-9

BREAKING ALL THE RULES

Copyright © 2007 by Harlequin Books S.A.

Carol I. Wagner and Marian L. Franz are acknowledged as the author of this work.

Dear Reader,

What woman wouldn't want to sail off on a Mediterranean cruise and meet a tall, handsome man who takes her breath away? Not many that we know of, and our heroine, Lola Sandler, is no exception. Unfortunately, there are some obstacles standing in the way of her experiencing the perfect romantic vacation. She's keeping secrets about her real reasons for seeking out the ship's golf pro, Eric Lashman—who has secrets of his own—and she's traveling with her mother and two sisters. Not the easiest way to conduct a shipboard romance.

There are many things going on in Lola's life at the moment. Her widowed mother is turning into a social butterfly right in front of her eyes. Her sisters are both having trouble with their love lives, and Lola's falling head over heels in love with the reclusive golf pro she's desperate to get an interview with.

Add to this the swirling undercurrents of danger and intrigue that surround certain members of *Alexandra's Dream*'s crew, exotic and breathtakingly beautiful ports of call, a terrorist attack with Lola and Eric caught in the middle of a hundred-year-old feud, and you have the makings of the trip of a lifetime—if you can survive it all.

Hope you enjoy reading *Breaking All the Rules* as much as Marian and I enjoyed writing it.

Bon voyage,

Carol Wagner and Marian Franz

DON'T MISS THE STORIES OF

Mediterranean
N I G H T S™

CHAPTER ONE

ALEXANDRA'S DREAM swayed gently at her moorings in the harbor at Monte Carlo. Nearly encircling the cruise ship, the lights of the harbor and, higher yet, those of the city, sparkled against the dark mass of hills that guarded the famed principality of Monaco.

"It really is like a fairy-tale world, isn't it? I'm glad our ship is too big to dock on the quay. The view from here is breathtaking, don't you think?"

"Gorgeous," Lola agreed with her sister, Bonnie. "And this ship's not half bad, either. We owe Marilyn a really special thank-you gift for booking us on her."

Myra Sandler sniffed. "Marilyn would never book us on a ship that was merely 'not half bad.'" Marilyn was Bonnie and Lola's mother's best friend, a travel agent in Sarasota, Florida, where the two women made their homes. "This ship is magnificent."

"I stand corrected," Lola apologized with a smile. Of

course her mother was right. *Alexandra's Dream* had only recently been refurbished by its new owner, the Greek shipping magnate, Elias Stamos, who had purchased the American Liberty Line and its three cruise ships. Like her sister ships, *Alexandra's Dream* had long sleek lines and a graceful clipper bow, spoiled only by the somewhat boxy look of her squared-off stern, the result of an increased number of cabins with balconies—on one of which Lola, her mother and sisters were sitting comfortably, if a little snugly, at this very moment.

Bonnie took a sip of club soda from her wineglass as she continued to scan the vista before them. The night was warm and quiet, the sky above the dark hills filled with a multitude of stars that were echoed in the silver and gold of the Liberty Line logo on the smokestack high overhead. "Is that building with the two big towers the casino?" Bonnie pointed toward the shore. "Or is it the cathedral? Or the royal palace? I'm confused."

"That's the casino," Lola explained. "The palace is over there across the harbor. And we can't see the cathedral from this angle."

"Which you would have known if you'd taken the city tour with us this afternoon. The casino was designed by the same architect who built the Paris Opera House." Lola's oldest sister, Frances, looked over the top of her half-glasses at Bonnie, her guide book open on the table before her. Even on vacation Fran tended to lapse into her middle-school-principal mode if she got half a chance.

"It was too hot and I was too jet-lagged," Bonnie defended herself. She set the wineglass on the small table. Unconsciously, she rested her hands on her stomach a moment, then abruptly folded them together on the tabletop. "You know how wiped out I get when I'm knocked up," she said in an unusually sharp voice.

Bonnie was expecting her fifth child at the end of February, a little less than seven months away. The announcement of her sister's pregnancy during a phone conversation a few weeks earlier had surprised Lola. She thought Bonnie and her husband, Tad, had called a halt after the birth of their fourth child, and only son, Alex, six years earlier.

"Besides," Bonnie added, "I wanted to see the oceanographic museum. I was the biggest Jacques Cousteau fan when I was a kid."

Lola didn't remember anything about her sisters' childhoods because they had both been in high school by the time she had any clear memories of them at all. Bonnie was ten years older than she was and Frances, who had just passed her fortieth birthday, was a year and a half older than Bonnie.

"Before my time."

Bonnie wrinkled her nose at Lola's teasing. "He was the director of the institute for years and years. I couldn't pass up a chance to see the place. And it was worth it. Didn't you think so, Mom?"

"It was interesting," Myra agreed, taking a sip of her wine. "Lots and lots of fish. Your father would have wanted to try to catch them, God rest his soul." Myra was short and small-boned, her figure softly rounded, her salt-and-pepper hair cut close to her head in a sophisticated bob.

Bonnie and Fran both took after their mother in size and coloring, although, neither was as plump as Myra and their dark hair held no hint of gray. Lola, on the other hand, was tall and slender with curly shoulder-

length blond hair and green eyes. She would have sometimes wondered if she wasn't the cuckoo in the nest if
she hadn't resembled her father in temperament as well
as looks. Walter Sandler had been gone almost four
years now but she still missed him very much.

"Thank goodness Bonnie couldn't buy fish for souvenirs," Fran broke in. "She's got half a suitcase full of soap
from Marseilles, already." The ten-day Western Mediterranean cruise they'd given their mother for a sixty-
fifth birthday present had originated in the French port
city the day before, and they'd been able to take a whirlwind shopping and sightseeing tour before embarking.

"Three euros for a kilo bar," Bonnie informed her
older sister. "French-milled. Scented with real Provence
lavender. I could have bought out the store. And where
else am I going to find such lovely, inexpensive presents
for Tad's mother and sisters?"

"The soap does smell lovely, dear," Myra said, patting Bonnie's hand. "And it was interesting to watch it
being made right there in front of us. I'm sure Tad's
mother and sisters will be thrilled with your choice. It
would have been interesting to visit the casino, too, but
it was simply too hot to bother with dressing appropriately to go inside," she concluded, segueing back to the
original subject with her final words.

"We were dressed appropriately for sightseeing,"
Bonnie chuckled. "Just not for rubbing shoulders with
the upper crust in Monte Carlo."

"That's what I said." Myra rolled her eyes at her
middle daughter and took another sip of wine. "What a
beautiful evening. What a beautiful view." She sighed
contentedly. "I could stay here all night."

Lola and her sisters exchanged satisfied glances.

The three of them had pooled their yearly dividend from their father's successful accounting firm, now run by their cousin, to pay for the trip. But it had been Marilyn who had gotten Myra's cabin upgraded to the premier stateroom on the Poseidon deck. Lola, Fran and Bonnie were sharing a much smaller cabin three decks below and much farther aft than Myra's spacious room with its seashell-pink and mother-of-pearl color scheme, twin beds, tiled bath and comfortable seating area.

"Are you sure one of you girls doesn't want to move in here with me?" Myra asked for at least the tenth time.

"No, Mom," Bonnie said hastily.

"Thanks. No."

"We're all settled in downstairs," Lola said, swallowing a giggle with a sip of wine. "Or belowdecks or however you say it."

Their cabin, while not as spacious as Myra's, was big enough that they didn't have to do a Three Stooges routine to get showered and dressed. It, too, had twin beds, with a third berth above one of the beds that folded away into the wall during the day. The cabin was decorated in a kind of French country style, Lola supposed you would call it. Yellow walls, white coverlets on the beds, blue-and-yellow-patterned draperies framing the picture window, which, unfortunately, opened onto a view of one of the lifeboats and not a heavenly balcony like the one where they were sitting.

"You don't all have to trip over each other turning down my offer. I know you don't want to sleep with me because I snore."

"No, Mom, it's not that at all," Bonnie, middle child, and always the peacemaker, assured Myra. "We want this to be just for you." She waved her hand at the suite beyond the sliding-glass door.

Across the table Lola avoided her oldest sister's eyes. Fran took a quick sip of wine and Myra snorted, waving one tanned, beringed hand in their general direction. "Oh, stop your silliness. I know perfectly well it's the snoring. You three couldn't pull the wool over my eyes when you were girls and you still can't. And just remember, I wouldn't snore if Frances hadn't hit me in the face with that softball and broken my nose all those years ago." She touched her finger to the tip of her nose, which was only the tiniest bit crooked.

"I was only eleven. And I want it on the record for the fiftieth time that you were the one who showed me how to put more 'English' on the ball," Fran protested.

"Well, it worked, didn't it," Myra said smugly. "You got a softball scholarship to Ohio State, didn't you?"

"Yes, mother. I will never forget. That's where I met Gary." Gary McKlimon was Fran's ex, the father of her twin teenage sons. They were long divorced but had remained friends. Lola wished she could say the same for herself and her ex-husband. She hadn't spoken to Jack Carson in the eight months since their divorce had become final, although they still lived in the same town. Frances upended her wineglass. "Is there any more of that lovely chardonnay left?"

"No, I'm afraid it's all gone, but wasn't it thoughtful of Marilyn to have arranged for it to be here when we came on board? She's such a good friend." Myra gave a little sniff and touched the corner of her eye as though to wipe away a tear. Not because she was upset about the snoring—it was a running joke between them…and their father, also, before his death. Nor was

she overwhelmed by her friend's gesture. It was just that
Myra tended to get very sentimental when she was tipsy,
and it didn't take much more than a glass of wine or
two to make it happen. "I swear, this is the best birthday
present I've ever recieved. Thank you, sweeties, thank
you very much."

"You're welcome, Momma."

"Love ya."

"Happy birthday, Mom, and many more," all three of
them chorused, raising their glasses in a toast. Bonnie
blew her mother a kiss. They weren't a touchy-feely
kind of family, which, at the moment, was a good thing,
because there wasn't much room to maneuver on the
narrow balcony, anyway.

"I could stay out here forever," Myra said with another little sniff of happy tears. "Really, I could."

Frances had gone back to perusing her guidebook
since no more wine was forthcoming.

"What's on the itinerary for tomorrow?" Bonnie
asked, standing to rest her hands on the gleaming white
railing and look out along the sides of the ship.

Laughter and soft conversations floated to them from
the verandas above and below, although, the ones on
either side appeared deserted at the moment. Their oc-
cupants must have opted for the early seating for dinner,
Lola surmised.

Fran closed her guidebook and took up the printed
sheet of paper that had been slipped under their cabin
door earlier that morning. "Day at sea," she read, perusing the single-spaced sheet. "Lots to do. All the usual.
Low-impact aerobics at 8:00 a.m."

"Scratch that," Lola interrupted without apology. "I'll
still be sleeping, or having coffee on the Lido deck or

whatever they call it on this ship. I refuse to exercise that early in the morning."

Fran ignored her complaint and kept reading. "Breakfast is served in the Empire Room and the Garden Terrace and Buffet beginning at seven. For early risers coffee and Continental breakfast is available at the pool deck bar from six until nine."

"Thanks. That sounds like just the ticket."

"What else is going on in the morning?" Myra asked curiously.

"Ballroom dancing with Señor Antonio Mendoza. That's at ten in La Belle Epoque. That's the nightclub, I believe."

"It's on the deck above our stateroom," Lola supplied. She'd checked it out the night before after her sisters had gone to bed. The ornately decorated room with its gold-and-black pillars, teak champagne bar and lit dance floor had been crowded even though a lot of the American passengers on the cruise must have been as jet-lagged as she was.

"Bacchus deck," Frances supplied, then kept on reading. "In the afternoon there's skeet shooting off the aft deck. Golf lessons with the ship's pro, Andrew Lashman. Ever heard of him, Lola?"

Lola was the sports editor for a medium-sized newspaper in a medium-sized Ohio city. Or she had been until her ex-husband, a college women's basketball coach, had gotten caught up in a steroid-abuse scandal. Now she edited the "Women's Page," as it was still called. Food articles, religion, entertainment and human-interest stories landed on her desk—everything, it seemed, but sports. The move was temporary, her boss had assured her. Until it all shook out with Jack.

The paper didn't want any conflict of interest, and neither did he. But that was three months ago, and the investigation was still dragging on…and she was still exiled among the recipes, housecleaning hints and makeup tips.

"I'm sorry. What did you say his name was again?" she asked Frances. Golf wasn't a sport she was particularly well versed in, but the name Lashman rang a faint bell in her memory.

"Andrew Lashman. He's South African according to his bio. Do you remember him from the orientation lecture yesterday?"

"I didn't go to orientation. I wasn't about to sit in a dark auditorium for two hours when the sun was so glorious out on deck."

"I was e-mailing the kids," Bonnie said, still with her back to them.

Fran made a tsking sound with her tongue. "It's always a good idea to attend the orientation lecture on a cruise, you should know that."

"That's what Marilyn says, too," Myra seconded.

"Since this is my first cruise," Bonnie retorted, "I suppose I can be excused for not knowing that."

"I'll have it tattooed on the back of my eyelids so I don't forget in the future," Lola promised.

Fran gave her a frown that struck fear into a thirteen-year-old's heart but no longer held such power over Lola…at least, not most of the time. She cleared her throat and sat up a little straighter in her chair. "Andrew Lashman, you said?"

"Cape Town, South Africa."

"Nope. Nothing."

"Tall, dark blond hair, kind of weathered-looking.

Midthirties, I'd say. Handsome in a kind of rough-hewn way. Great accent." Myra stood and started gathering up the wineglasses and the empty bottle. "I signed up for a lesson tomorrow. As a matter of fact, I signed Lola up, too."

"Mom," Lola protested. "I hate golf. You know I can't hit a straight ball to save my life."

"You could if you'd get serious about it. You're an excellent athlete and always have been. Besides, I don't want to go alone."

"What do you need lessons for? You've got a twelve handicap." Myra had been her senior league champ two years running.

"It's free and he's cute," Myra said.

All three of her daughters blinked in surprise. Lola felt her mouth fall open and shut it quickly. She shot Fran a questioning look. Her older sister shrugged. Their father had died suddenly and unexpectedly of a massive stroke four years earlier. One minute he had been there, serious, work-driven but always their rock, and the next he was gone. Myra had taken his death very hard and mourned him sincerely. And until this very moment she had never mentioned so much as a passing interest in any other man, old or young.

In fact, Lola and her sisters had had to do a lot of fast talking to get Myra to agree to come on the cruise at all. Since her husband's death, her world had contracted to her friends at the senior condo complex where she lived in Sarasota, her grandchildren and golf and charity work. She insisted she was happy the way she was, but Lola, Bonnie and Fran had disagreed. The cruise was their latest attempt to bring their mother out of her shell. Evidently it was working.

"I think I'll take in the lecture on Etruscan art and architecture in the library at ten," Fran said. "It's being given by Father Patrick Connelly. It says here he's a fellow of the American Archeological Society and was associated with the Vatican Etruscan museum for two years." She looked over the top of her glasses once more. "How about joining me, Bonnie?"

"Sounds too much like self-improvement to be fun," Bonnie said noncommittally. "I'll let you know in the morning." She was still standing at the rail. Lola watched her sister in profile. She was frowning slightly and had been very quiet ever since they'd met at the Newark airport for their flight to France. At first, Lola had thought it was jet lag and the strain of traveling in the August heat. Now she wasn't so sure. Bonnie was tense and quiet, not her usual easy-going, fun-loving self. Surely her pregnancy was progressing normally or she wouldn't have taken the risk of traveling to Europe. Still, she was thirty-eight. Being pregnant again had to be a strain.

"There's a rock-climbing wall. I think I'm going to try that tomorrow morning," Lola said, scanning the sheet she'd plucked from Fran's grasp. "And then I'm going to sit by the pool and drink…whatever the special of the day happens to be."

"That sounds like more fun than a lecture on Etruscan art, even if I can't drink," Bonnie said, turning to rest her hip against the railing. "I'll come along and watch."

"I've also signed up for the ballroom-dancing lessons with Señor Mendoza if anyone cares to join me," Myra announced, cradling the empty wine bottle in the crook of her elbow as she opened the glass slider to enter the cabin.

Lola's eyes widened. "Ballroom dancing?"

"Yes, I've wanted to try it ever since I watched that TV show *Dancing With the Stars* or whatever it was called."

"And let me guess," Lola began, "Señor What's-his-name is also a very good-looking man."

"Yes. As is Father Connelly. Right, Frances?" Myra glanced at her watch, not waiting for her eldest daughter to reply. "Goodness, look at the time. We'd better hurry and change or we'll miss our dinner seating. I checked out the menu earlier this afternoon. I'm going to have the spring lamb with the parmesan rosemary crust. And there's mango crème brûlée on the dessert menu. I love crème brûlée."

"Father Connelly?" Lola mouthed the words. "She's checking out a priest?"

Fran took the newsletter from Lola and used it as a bookmark as she shut her guidebook and stood. "He's a dead ringer for Spencer Tracy in *Bad Day at Black Rock*," she whispered as they followed their mother into the suite.

Lola didn't need any more of a description. She could easily picture the famous opening scene of the classic movie with the craggy-faced actor in his dark suit and black fedora getting off the train in the middle of the one-horse, desert town. One thing all the Sandler women shared was a love of old movies.

"What is it? Something in the air? The wine?" Lola was genuinely puzzled.

"Do you think she's doing all this stuff just to show us she appreciates us giving her the cruise for her birthday?" Bonnie asked. "I mean, she is sixty-five. I don't want her to overdo it."

Fran snorted. "She's as strong as an ox. No, that's

not it. Maybe she just thinks it's time to end her mourn-ing for Dad."

"Well, that's what we wanted, right?" Lola felt a lit-tle pang of guilt and disloyalty to her dead father, but did her best to banish it. Her mother was too young and vital for her daughters to want her to spend the rest of her life alone.

"Right." Fran nodded but the response lacked her usual self-assurance. "I guess."

CHAPTER TWO

LOLA LEANED BACK in the plastic chair and popped a sweet purple grape into her mouth. She chewed and swallowed, letting the taste of the tart juice linger on her tongue, then took a bite of her buttery croissant. So far the food aboard *Alexandra's Dream* had been heavenly. She was afraid she was going to gain far more than the three pounds she'd told herself she could handle without rejoining the health club. She closed her eyes and turned her face to the sun for a moment before picking up her coffee cup and taking a sip of the strong, dark liquid.

"I'm sorry you missed your chance to climb the rock wall," Bonnie said. She was sitting across the table from Lola, a big floppy straw hat shading her fair skin from the Mediterranean sun that Lola was soaking up. Fran and Bonnie burned and peeled and rarely worked up a tan even at the end of summer. Lola tanned easily and never burned badly enough to peel, another characteristic inherited from their father that both her sisters envied.

"I've got all week to try it," Lola said, but promised herself she'd check out the exercise facilities on the ship so she wouldn't have to wave off the dessert trolley when it came around that evening. She scanned the selection of fruit on her plate, picked up a slice of orange and took a bite. "It's too hot now, anyway. Besides, I'd much rather sit here with you." They were seated at one of twenty or so small round tables beneath a canvas awning outside the Garden Terrace. It was late morning and the breakfast buffet had just closed. Behind them, the sounds of china and glassware being moved around and conversations in half a dozen languages filtered through the open glass sliders as the friendly and efficient food-service crew reset the long buffet for the lunch crowd.

Bonnie rolled her eyes. "The same way you'd rather sit in the cabin with me this morning while I barfed my guts out in the bathroom instead of having a real breakfast and getting your climb in?"

"I didn't mind, really. And I'm having breakfast right now. A lot healthier breakfast than if I'd grazed through the buffet. I can't pass up anything that looks good, or even interesting. You know that." Her sister's bout of morning sickness had been intense but, thankfully, short-lived. "You're feeling better now, aren't you?" Lola asked, trying to sound less worried than she really was. Bonnie's face looked pinched and tired, and her blue eyes were shadowed with worry. She hadn't slept well, Lola knew. Her sister's tossing and turning in the bed below her had kept her awake for a long time after they'd turned out the lights.

"Just peachy." Bonnie crumbled a cracker onto her

plate. Lola noticed her hands were shaking and her worry ratcheted up a notch or two.

"You weren't this sick with Alex or the girls," Lola ventured. Bonnie and Tad's daughters were redheaded stair steps, twelve, eleven and nine years old. They got their red hair from their father's family and their sunny dispositions from their mother. Alex had Lola's coloring and eyes the same shade of green, as well as his father's sturdy build. Lola loved her nieces, but her hellion nephew was secretly her favorite. Bonnie had always boasted being pregnant was the easiest job she'd ever had. It was raising the babies after they were born that took its toll on a woman.

"I'm seven years older than I was when I was carrying Alex." She pushed her cup of weak tea away with a grimace. "The truth is I feel a hundred and seven years older," she said, avoiding looking directly at Lola.

"You're okay, aren't you? The baby's okay?" Some of the anxiety Lola was feeling seeped into her words. She propped her elbows on the table and studied her sister's drawn features. "Tad wouldn't have let you come if there was any danger for you or the baby."

To her surprise and distress, tears welled up in her sister's eyes. "Of course not. Tad would never let me put myself or our babies at risk." Lola's brother-in-law was a great father. He was a fireman and a paramedic for a town north of Sarasota. On the days he was off duty at the fire department, he took over the household chores so that Bonnie could work in the admissions department of an area nursing home.

Lola relaxed a little. "I thought not. But come on, something's bothering you and I don't think it's just morning sickness."

"I— I'm just tired, that's all."

Her tone wasn't convincing and Lola wasn't satisfied with the answer. She opened her mouth to refute Bonnie's assurance, but a shadow fell across the table. Lola looked up, annoyed to have their conversation interrupted. Her gaze met the smiling eyes of a priest in a black, short-sleeved shirt and Roman collar, who was, indeed, the spitting image of Spencer Tracy in his later years. He was accompanied by a pleasant-looking woman about her sister's age.

The woman held out her hand. "Welcome aboard. I'm Patti Kennedy, the cruise director, and this is Father Patrick Connelly. He's our guest lecturer. He'll be giving a series of talks on Mediterranean art and history during the cruise."

"Ladies, welcome aboard." There was the slightest hint of an Irish brogue underlying his words, although the tiny U.S. flag emblem on his name tag proclaimed his citizenship to be American, as was Patti Kennedy's. The former owners of the cruise line had been American, and a lot of the crew had stayed with the company when it was taken over by its Greek owners, Marilyn had told them when they were making their travel arrangements.

"I'm Lola Sandler and this is my sister, Bonnie Kanine. Nice to meet both of you."

The priest's grip was firm and steady, his eyes retaining their friendly sparkle as he shook hands. "I hope you're enjoying yourselves, so far, aboard *Alexandra's Dream*."

"Yes, we're having a wonderful time," Lola responded as politely as she could manage.

"Will you be with us for the full three-week cruise?" Patti asked.

"No, I'm afraid not. My oldest sister is a school principal. She has to be back in her office for the beginning of the semester. We'll be leaving the ship after we dock in Venice."

"I'm sure you'll thoroughly enjoy the time you spend with us. If there's any way I can be of service while you're on board, please don't hesitate to contact me."

"Thank you. I'll remember that," Lola told her.

She just wished the woman and the smiling priest would go away so she could talk to her sister. Bonnie was still blinking hard as though she might burst into tears at any moment. Lola knew pregnant women were sometimes highly emotional, but she'd seen Bonnie pregnant a lot of times over the last decade and she'd never once burst into tears for any reason, happy or sad.

Patti Kennedy shook Bonnie's hand and Lola noticed a frown mar her friendly demeanor for a split second as she, too, saw the obvious distress on Bonnie's face. Father Connelly extended his hand. When Bonnie took it he covered it with both his own. "Sandler," he said. "There was a lovely lady and her daughter who signed up for my lecture series this morning. They both looked a great deal like you." He turned his head toward Lola and his bonhomie faltered just a bit.

She smiled despite her annoyance at their interruption. "But not like me. I take after my dad, Father Connelly."

"A lucky man to have such charming daughters," he said smoothly. "Your mother mentioned her youngest was a dead ringer for the bust of Aphrodite she saw among my small collection of Greek and Etruscan reproductions on display in the ship's library."

"You'll have to excuse my mother. She's prejudiced

in my favor." Lola was chagrined to feel a blush creeping over her cheeks.

Father Connelly gave a courtly little dip of his head. "On the contrary, she was right on the money. You'll have to stop by and see the bust for yourself."

"As I mentioned before, if there's anything I can do to make your stay aboard ship more pleasant, please let me know," Patti Kennedy interjected with a smile. "We want our passengers to be happy."

"Thank you," Lola replied politely. *Now go away,* she said to herself. *I need to find out why my pregnant sister is on the verge of crying her eyes out in public.*

"Good day, ladies," Father Connelly said, as though Patti Kennedy's words were a prearranged signal. Farewells were exchanged and they moved toward a table occupied by a honeymoon couple who didn't look any more pleased to be interrupted at their late breakfast than Lola had been.

Bonnie went back to crumbling the dry crackers on her plate. "Fran was right. He's the spitting image of Spencer Tracy. It's amazing. I almost couldn't stop myself from saying something. I bet he gets tired of hearing it." Bonnie was rambling, talking fast and breathlessly to keep Lola from reverting to their earlier subject. "I wonder what he's doing on a cruise? I mean, shouldn't he be taking care of his flock back in the States somewhere?"

"Not all priests have churches. Maybe he's on some kind of sabbatical or vacation or something." Lola reached out and touched the back of her sister's hand, stilling her restless fingers. "I don't care about him. I'm worried about you. Bonnie, what's troubling you? You haven't been yourself since we met at the airport. You can tell me. Is there something wrong at home?"

"No." Tears leaked out of the corners of her sister's eyes. "Yes. Something is wrong. It's me. It's this baby."

"You just said you were fine. Healthy as an ox, you told Mom. I heard you."

"I am healthy. At least, physically. It's in my heart I'm sick." She put her fingertips to her lips as though to stop the words she was about to speak. "Oh, Lola Roly-Pola, don't make me dump this on you," she begged, using the pet name she had bestowed on Lola when she and Fran had first set eyes on the plump and red-faced infant their mother had brought home from the hospital for them to fuss over like a new doll.

Lola wasn't about to be put off so easily. "If you don't tell me what's wrong, I'm going straight back to the cabin to put in an overseas call to Tad this very minute."

"No!" More tears leaked from the corners of Bonnie's eyes. Lola grabbed a napkin and held it out to her sister.

"Are you and Tad having problems?" Tad and Bonnie had been in love since eighth grade. Her brother-in-law had been a part of their family as long as Lola could remember.

"Yes." Bonnie wiped at the tears on her cheeks and refused to meet Lola's eyes, focusing her gaze on her left earlobe, instead. "As a matter of fact, we're not speaking."

"Why?" All kinds of scenarios hurtled through Lola's mind. Another woman? Another man? Lola rejected both possibilities as soon as they occurred to her. Whatever the problem was, it wasn't infidelity, she'd bet her life on it. Behavior problems with the kids? Too much stress? Not enough communication? Tad's job involved long hours, dangerous situations and never enough money. Even with the dividend check the sisters received each year from Sandler and Associates, CPAs, none of them were wealthy. They all worked hard and sometimes juggled bills just like everyone else, but with four children and another on the way, Bonnie's situation was more precarious than Lola's or Fran's.

Giving their mother this cruise was a bigger sacrifice for Bonnie. That must be it. Lola relaxed a little. She had a few thousand dollars put away for a new car. She could loan it to Bonnie and Tad until the end of the year, help take the strain off. "Is it money? Has the fire department had its budget cut again? I can imagine what a hassle that must be with a new baby coming—"

"It's not money." Bonnie cut her off. "At least, not entirely," she said in a rush. "We never planned for another baby. We need a bigger house. The van's got 200,000 miles on it. We haven't put any money into the kids' education accounts for two years. And now I'm knocked up again. It was an accident, Lola. We got careless. I'm almost forty. I thought I was close enough to the change to be safe." She shrugged. "How stupid can you be? Me, the Fertility Queen of Hyacinth Lake, Florida." She took a deep breath and faced Lola head-on. "I might as well tell you straight out, but you have to swear you won't breathe a word to Fran or Mom. Especially not to Mom. Promise?"

Against her better judgment Lola nodded her head. All she wanted at the moment was to know what was making her sister so miserable. She would wrangle with her conscience later when she told Fran about this conversation, as she fully intended to do. "I promise."

Bonnie took a deep breath. She spoke barely above a whisper, but the words resonated in Lola's head as though her sister had stood on the table and shouted at the top of her lungs. "I'm not sure I'm going to go through with this pregnancy."

CHAPTER THREE

ERIC LASHMAN hated what he was doing. He wondered how his brother, Andrew, put up with it day in and day out. The smiles, the handshakes, the endless discussions about a game he never wanted to play professionally again. He stood at the rail watching Patti Kennedy and the priest work the crowd on the aft deck outside the buffet. Patti Kennedy was a pro at her job and a genuinely likable woman. The priest, he wasn't so sure about, jovial and outgoing on the surface, yes, but there were times when they met belowdecks that Eric noticed a hardness around his mouth and a coldness in his eyes that were at odds with his hale-fellow-well-met persona.

He wasn't just being paranoid. He'd spent half his life learning to read expressions and body language. It told you so much about your opponent. Golf was cerebral, a game of nuance, of inches and, to stay on top, you had to use every advantage you could get. But he wasn't on top of the game anymore. He was out of it. For good and for all.

He halted the unwelcome inward turn of his thoughts and directed his attention to the table where Patti and Father Connelly were engaged in conversation with a pair of passengers. At the moment it looked like the cruise director and the priest might have met their match in the tall, lithe blonde and her shorter, plumper companion seated at the small glass-topped table. The blond woman was polite but her smile was strained and he could tell she wasn't happy to have her conversation, or perhaps it was her breakfast, interrupted.

As Eric watched, the priest took the darker woman's hand between both his own, his smile at full voltage. Father Pat Connelly was something else. A priest who was on sabbatical, or whatever the church called a leave of absence, to rest and recuperate after years of teaching at a school for disadvantaged boys somewhere in the Midwestern United States. Not only did the man look like Spencer Tracy, but evidently he was the living embodiment of the actor's *Boys Town* persona.

Eric had seen the movie once or twice years ago when he was a kid and his dad had been swinging the clubs well and brought them home a big color TV with the money he'd made hustling tourists at the local course in Cape Town. The TV had been one of the biggest in their shabby neighborhood and his and Andrew's best friend—a reminder of the home in North Carolina they'd left behind after their American mother's death, a continuous source of voices and laughter and familiar old sitcoms to comfort two homesick boys in this strange country that was now their home.

While he'd been lost in his thoughts, Patti and the

priest had moved on. That was his cue to follow. Time to hawk the golf lessons he—or rather his younger brother—was paid to sell to the cruise patrons, along with golf outings at the various ports of call, where some of the greens fees were pretty expensive. But Liberty Line catered to a well-heeled clientele, mostly American and British with a smattering of Asian and European thrown in for good measure, and money wasn't an object to most of them.

He settled the dark blue Liberty Line sun visor more firmly on his head and pulled the stack of brochures he was supposed to hand out from the back pocket of his slacks. At least he felt comfortable in his uniform of dark blue collared shirt and khaki slacks. They were pretty much the same kind of clothes he'd worn for eight years on the pro tour.

A middle-aged British couple he'd met at dinner at the captain's table the night before came up to him and asked for a brochure. He stood, legs braced against the gentle roll of the ship, talking with them for a moment, discussing the courses that were available to play in Rome and Naples, their two overnight ports of call, and jotting down the hours he would be at the Shore Excursion desk so they could sign up for the outings they wanted to take. By the time they'd sauntered off toward the buffet he noticed the blond woman and her companion had been joined by two more women. The dark trio had to be mother and sisters, he surmised, walking toward them. But the blonde? Half sister? Cousin? Friend?

He narrowed his eyes, watching the women for a few more seconds before moving to join them. No, not friend. There were too many similarities in the way they all laughed and smiled, but the blonde was very different from the others. Cousin, more likely, or the child of a second marriage, perhaps? She was tall and slender, athletic-looking and younger than the others by at least a decade.

"Ladies," he said, touching his finger to the bill of the sun visor as he came abreast of their table. "Good morning. I hope you're enjoying your cruise so far."

The oldest of the quartet, the mother, obviously, smiled up at him from her seat. "We are having a wonderful time," she said with the flat twang that announced a middle-America upbringing, although the deep tan and tiny lines fanning out from her eyes suggested she spent most of her time somewhere warmer and sunnier, Arizona or Florida, perhaps.

"Gorgeous weather," said the woman who had arrived with her.

He glanced at the daughter who had been sitting at the table when he first became aware of them. She wasn't having a good time. She'd been crying. He'd seen the blonde offer her a napkin to wipe her eyes and there were still traces of tears on her cheeks. "Very nice." She didn't meet his eyes.

"And you?" he couldn't help asking. He'd seen the tenseness in the blonde's neck and shoulders as she'd talked to the priest and the cruise director, the barely concealed impatience that they be on their way and leave her alone with the unhappy woman.

"Great," she muttered. The sun was behind him but he doubted that was the only reason she narrowed her eyes when she glanced up at him. She wasn't any happier to see him than she had been Patti and Father Connelly.

"I'm glad to hear that." He held out his hand. "I'm Eric Lashman, the golf pro."

From the corner of his eye he saw the blonde's eyes widen. "Eric Lashman," she repeated softly. He felt his gut tighten momentarily.

Had she recognized him? His name was hardly a household word in the States or Britain. He'd been on the pro tour eight seasons and won two majors, but he wasn't Tiger Woods by a long shot, and he'd been out of the limelight for four years, a lifetime in the world of professional golf. But he'd known it was only a matter of time before some golf fanatic figured out who he was—or more precisely who he had once been.

The dark sister with the half glasses pushed up in her hair spoke. "The brochure says your name's Andrew Lashman."

"My brother. He was called home for a family emergency." He smiled, calling on the iron control he'd developed to hide his emotions from the sharks that trolled the greens and fairways of the pro tours around the globe, looking for that one little weakness, that chink in the armor they could exploit. "I'm taking his place for a few weeks."

Andrew's longtime girlfriend had given birth to their first child prematurely a month earlier. Both mother and baby were doing fine, even though his niece weighed just shy of two kilos, but Andrew wanted to stay with them for a few weeks more. And the only way the cruise line would hold his job for him was if he supplied a suitable replacement. "And who could be more suitable than my big brother, the world famous tour pro?" he'd said to Eric.

"Just about anyone who can swing a club," Eric had replied. "You know I'm a lousy instructor. I haven't got the patience."

Andrew did have the patience and the ability to teach others the fundamentals of a good golf game. Eric didn't. He was an instinctive golfer with a good work ethic and the kind of build and dexterity it took to swing a golf club, not a natural like his brother. But beneath Andrew's teasing Eric had sensed his anxiety to get home to Angela and the baby, so he had said yes, even though it was the last thing in the world he'd wanted to do. Since their hard-drinking and hard-living father's death, Andrew was the only family he had left and, after all these years of being Andrew's big brother, he couldn't quit now.

"Eric Lashman. I've heard of you." The blonde's voice washed over him like smoke and honey. He turned his head and found himself staring into sea-green eyes. Not the turquoise of the Mediterranean, but the cool, clear green of the Atlantic where he'd surfed as a teenager, always on the lookout for the great white sharks that made the coast of South Africa their home and hunting grounds. "You won the Open in—" Her eyes narrowed slightly in concentration.

"A long time ago," he said quietly. Inwardly he winced. She knew something about golf or she would have made the layman's mistake of calling it the British Open. Well, it had to happen sooner or later. He'd been on board nearly three weeks. Someone was bound to recognize him eventually.

The well-preserved matriarch held out her hand. "I'm Myra Sandler and these are my daughters, Frances, Bonnie and Lola."

Lola. That was the youngest one. The outlier. The rebel in the family, he'd bet. The name suited her. Half ordinary, half exotic, depending on whether it was spoken in passion or in anger. She looked like that, too, ordinary, wholesome in white shorts and a white shirt with a V-neck and little cap sleeves, curly blond hair pulled up in an untidy knot on top of her head. Yet the toenails peeking out of her sandals were painted watermelon-pink and her dangling earrings were tiny gold flamingos. But it was her eyes that fascinated him most. Cool, calculating on the surface, but if you looked deeply enough you could see they swirled with a kind of inner fire that hinted at passion trapped deep inside.

Eric pulled himself together. Where the hell had that come from? He never waxed poetic like that about a woman's eyes. Especially not one who was glowering at him as though she might bite off his head any moment.

"I saw you win the Buick Open five years ago." Myra Sandler was still speaking. "I mean, I watched on television. I can't believe we're lucky enough to have you on the cruise. I've already signed up for lessons. I'm trying to talk my daughter into joining me." She motioned toward Lola with a plump hand that had a ring on almost every finger.

"I'm glad to hear that," he lied, touching the visor once more. He needed to get moving again. To get beyond the range of those curious, intelligent green eyes before she dredged up the memory of him walking off the green at Augusta that April Saturday afternoon, and that's where her thoughts were headed, he could tell. Lola Sandler, or whatever her name might be, was trouble. He could sense it with every competition-honed nerve in his body.

"I doubt they have clubs I can use," Lola said, turning her green eyes on her mother, freeing him to take a long, steadying breath.

"Lola's left-handed," Myra Sandler explained. "Do you have a set of left-handed women's clubs on board?"

"I believe we do," he said, taking the chance of looking directly into those green eyes once more.

"Excellent," the mother said, beaming. Her voice seemed to come from a long way away. "I'll make sure both our names are registered immediately after lunch."

It took most of his willpower to break contact with those sexy cat eyes and turn his head toward the older woman. "I'll be at the Shore Excursion desk from two until three-thirty. We can take care of the paperwork then. Nice meeting all of you," he said, lying again, and walked away.

"LET'S GO. There's nothing here I want to buy and it's too beautiful an afternoon to spend inside." Lola led the way out of one of the ship's boutiques into the broad corridor of the Bacchus deck, with its large recessed windows filled with flowers and objets d'art, framed by the blue Mediterranean. They'd been window-shopping while Myra and Bonnie were at Myra's ballroom-dancing lessons. "How about cocktails on the pool deck?" Lola asked as they headed for the elevators. "I'm buying."

Fran walked beside her. "All right," she agreed, then stopped in front of a closed door with a neatly lettered brass sign. "Hey, here's the library. Let's look inside."

It was Lola's turn to frown. "Do we have to? There's an empty deck chair and a Grey Goose martini with my name on it up there somewhere."

"We're right here and I just want to take a peek," Fran insisted. She opened the door and stepped inside. The library was a pleasant, lamplit room with big, comfortable leather chairs and shelves of books. One or two people sat in the chairs, reading newspapers and magazines. Several more were studying the lighted, glass-fronted shelves that held a dozen or so pieces of what appeared to be Greek and Roman art. Father Connelly, in clerical black and Roman collar, was playing host to the browsers.

The white-haired priest turned and smiled as they entered. "Good afternoon," he said. "It's good to see you again." He gestured to the articles behind the glass. "My pride and joy."

Coming closer, Lola could see the collection was more extensive and from a more varied time period than she had first supposed. Sitting among the wine jars and Roman coins was a small statue of the Egyptian cat goddess, Bast, she thought it might be called, a frieze of Greek athletes, naked and buff, a winged lion and a couple of small votive heads of warriors, or poets or maybe even gods and goddesses. History had never been her strong point.

"I bet you came to see my bust of Aphrodite," the priest said jovially. "It's one of my favorites. The one your mother thinks looks like you and, I have to say, I agree." Pride was evident in the priest's voice and in his body language. It struck Lola as rather odd that a man of God should be so focused on worldly things. Weren't priests supposed to be above that kind of weakness? She gave herself a little mental kick. He was a human being. Even priests were allowed to have hobbies and interests beyond their ecclesiastical duties.

Lola moved closer to the display cases, her steps dragging. Might as well get it over with. If she didn't take a look at the statue now, her mother would drag her back here the first chance she got, anyway. He pointed to a small marble bust of a woman with sightless eyes and intricately braided hair. Lola felt the hair on the back of her neck rise. The woman was not beautiful by any stretch of the imagination, but her face was strong and arresting and it did give Lola something of the sensation of looking into a distorted mirror. The feeling was unsettling, to say the least.

"It's spooky," she said, speaking the first words that came into her mind.

"It is a striking resemblance," the priest agreed. "Are you sure you don't have any Mediterranean ancestors in your family tree?"

"Positive."

"Well, that makes it even more interesting, doesn't it?" He clasped his hands behind his back and rocked on his heels. "A real puzzle."

A tall woman with a swimmer's lithe body rose from behind a big desk set between two windows at the far end of the room. She walked toward them. "Hi, I'm Ariana Bennett," she said, smiling. She was about Lola's age, maybe a few years older, with wavy brunette hair and vivid blue eyes framed by reading glasses. "I'm the ship's librarian. If you want to sign up for Father Connelly's lecture series I can do it for you."

"Thanks," Fran said, "but I'm already registered."

"But not this young lady. It's not too late. There are a few empty seats." The priest smiled coaxingly. "We start in just over an hour."

"I'll think about it," Lola murmured politely. In an hour she intended to be sitting by the pool with a drink in her hand.

"Father Connelly gives an excellent talk. He explains all the details of each of the artifacts. They're reproductions, but some of them are quite remarkable.

I'm sure you'd be glad you came." The enthusiasm in
the librarian's voice wasn't echoed in her eyes, Lola noticed. She wondered if Ariana Bennett got the same
slightly off-kilter vibes she experienced around the
priest, but didn't ask.

"They're all reproductions, but excellent ones."
His genial tone had hardened slightly. "One of my favorite pieces was broken by a careless steward a short
time ago. An amphora. Greek. Third century B.C." He
pointed to an empty shelf with a museum-type post-
card sitting on a small easel. "You see how lovely it
was."

Fran settled her glasses on the bridge of her nose and
peered closer. "The colors are beautiful, don't you
think so, Lola?"

Lola wrinkled her nose but held her tongue. The figures on the vessel were naked, too, like the warriors, but
they just looked silly to her, cavorting around the vase.

Fran was obviously more impressed. "Third century
B.C. So long ago. Yet they left such wonderful things
behind."

"I agree entirely," the priest said enthusiastically.
"The original of this piece is in a private collection." He
gave a rough little laugh. "But when it was broken, I felt
as bad as though it had really been a priceless relic in
pieces on the floor."

He was looking at Ariana, who flushed slightly.
"That's why I make sure that everything's safely locked
away before I close the library every night, Father. And
it was an accident, no one's fault."

"Yes, yes. An accident. I have the remains. I may try
to have it mended but I'm afraid it will never be display-
able again."

The harshness was gone, the smooth good humor back in his tone, but for Lola the assurance didn't ring true.

"If there's anything else I can do for you, don't hesitate to ask," Ariana said, changing the subject as she bent slightly to pick up a pile of discarded magazines from a side table. Lola caught sight of a copy of *Golf Digest*.

"There is one thing," she said. "Can you tell us how to get to the Internet café? I need to Google something."

Ariana's smile was less strained. "Check out the competition, you mean?" She gestured around the gracious, book-lined room with a sweep of her hand. "Our reference library is small, but excellent."

"I'm afraid I need the Internet," Lola apologized.

"Of course," Ariana's smile was polite and professional. "You're almost there. Just down the corridor. There's a sign on the door."

"IT IS HIM," Lola said, clicking out of the search window she'd opened on the PC in the ship's Internet café. "Eric Lashman. I knew I recognized the name. Then, when Mom fingered him for winning the Buick Open and the British Open, I got to thinking what else it was about him I remembered."

"What are you muttering about?" Fran asked, peering around the small partition that separated their flat-screen monitors. The communications center on *Alexandra's Dream*'s communications center was small but the equipment was all new and up-to-date.

"Eric Lashman. I knew I remembered something more about him than what Mom came up with this morning. I'm not that great a golf fan, but Jack was."

Fran made a face. "Every time you mention Jack's

name in that tone of voice I feel I need to make the sign of the cross to ward off the curse."

"Not everyone gets along with their ex as well as you do," Lola said. Fran had just sent off a two-page e-mail of instructions for her ex-husband regarding their twin sons, who were staying with him for the summer.

"Got along," Fran said, two deep furrows appearing between her eyebrows. "This business of the boys moving in with him to finish high school is putting a strain on our relationship."

"You know, I think it's a good idea they go with their dad." They'd had this discussion on the flight from Indianapolis to New Jersey and again from Newark to Marseilles. "Gary's a great guy. I don't know why you divorced him in the first place. He sure wasn't a Neanderthal rat like Jack."

"We fought all the time when we were married, you know that."

"I know he wanted to move out of the inner city, Fran, and give the boys the advantages he was working so hard to afford for them."

"And I want to stay where I'm at. If the administrators don't have faith in their schools and neighborhoods, who will?" Fran asked.

It was an old argument between them and one that Lola didn't want to resurrect at the moment. "Forget Gary and Jack. It's our ship's golf pro I'm interested in right now. Mom probably didn't recall what happened to him because it was so soon after Dad died and she was too depressed to be interested in anything, including golf. But Eric Lashman is the guy who walked off the twelfth green at Augusta four years ago during the Masters. He was six strokes ahead of the pack in the third round, and he just turned his back on an easy three-foot putt for a birdie that would have put him up seven and walked off the course. He withdrew from the tournament and the tour and, as far as I know, was never heard from again until today."

Fran came around the partition and looked at the picture on the screen. It was a younger, less hard-edged version of the man they'd met earlier, and he was smiling a smile that made Lola's toes curl as he doffed his hat to an unseen gallery. No wonder she'd had such a strong reaction to him outside the buffet a couple of hours ago. The man had sex appeal and charisma oozing out of every pore and she'd been celibate way too long. Two years at least. She and Jack hadn't had much of a love life the last six months of their marriage. She was bound to be vulnerable to a smile like that. To shoulders like that. To a butt like that— She pulled her thoughts away from sex and slammed the door on her suddenly resurrected libido.

"That's him, all right," Fran agreed. "And he's even better-looking now than when this was taken, don't you think?"

"I hadn't noticed," Lola fibbed.

"Well, I sure have," Fran admitted without guile. "That man is seriously sexy. Why do you suppose he did that?" she asked, thankfully dropping the subject of Eric Lashman's sex appeal. "You know, just walk away from all that money and fame and disappear?"

"I don't know, but I intend to find out." Lola clicked off the Internet and stood up, stretching her arms over her head.

"Lola, you aren't thinking of attempting to interview him for a newspaper article, are you?" Fran was frowning again, giving her the big-sister-disapproves look she'd perfected some twenty-nine years earlier.

"Why not?" Lola retorted, a shade more defensive than she wanted to sound. "'Where Are They Now?' stories are always good copy. It might even get picked up by the wire services. Or I could try to sell it to *Golf Digest* or something."

"You should drop this crazy notion because it's obvious the man doesn't want to be found, that's why. I saw how uncomfortable he looked when Mom brought up his wins on the tour. He didn't want to be outed. You should let him alone."

"No way. Patsy Carmichael is back home in Dayton tracking down leads to that steroid use by the women's basketball team at Dayton State that's liable to lead right back to my rat ex-husband. She'll probably end up with a Sports Writers Guild award. That should have been my story. My shot at the big time. Ex-husband or no ex-husband. Instead, I get exiled to the Women's Page. And now I'm floating around the Mediterranean with you and Mom and Bonnie threatening to have an abortion instead of another niece or nephew for us to spoil."

"What?" The color drained out of Fran's face, leaving a smattering of freckles standing out against her skin. Lola shut her mouth so quickly her teeth snapped together. She hadn't meant to just blurt it out that way. Fran reached out and caught Lola's wrist as though to keep her from running away. "What did you say about Bonnie having an—" she swallowed hard and, when she spoke again, the word came out in a cracked whisper "—an abortion?" Fran was a feminist from way back. She was pro choice all the way. But this was different. This was Bonnie. Her sister. The baby she was thinking of not having was Fran's flesh and blood. When the abstract became concrete, your most heartfelt convictions could turn on a dime. Lola knew, because that's what had happened to her three hours earlier.

This wasn't the way she'd wanted to tell her sister about Bonnie's predicament, but there were times she spoke before she thought, and this was one of them. She wasn't sorry for breaking her word to Bonnie. This was too important for her to keep from Fran. Sisters didn't keep secrets like that from each other, but she could have been more subtle, more gentle. "Come on, let's get out of here. I'll buy you an iced cappuccino and tell you all about it before Mom and Bonnie get back from Mom's ballroom-dancing lesson." She linked her arm through Fran's, relieved that she could unburden herself to her oldest sister. Fran was her surrogate mother, her best friend. She needed her counsel and her levelheaded advice. The intriguing puzzle of Eric Lashman, the sexy, disappearing golf pro, would have to wait. Family came first.

CHAPTER FOUR

FATHER PATRICK CONNELLY, a.k.a. Michael O'Connor, tugged at the stiff white collar that circled his throat as he stood at the end of the bar in La Belle Epoque, nursing his single-malt Scotch. He couldn't wait to get back to his cabin and change into something more comfortable. Comfortable, but conservative. He wasn't about to blow his cover at this stage of the game. He'd been on board *Alexandra's Dream,* masquerading as a priest, for almost four months now. It was a pretty sweet gig, all things considered. All those years spent in the purgatory of a Catholic school were finally paying off, just like the wasted two years at Nôtre Dame, where, unbelievably enough, the only classes he'd really enjoyed had been Greek and Roman history and the theater group he'd joined because it was a great place to meet rich coeds. Who would have thought they'd be the two talents he'd use to make his way in life?

Too bad the Hollywood stiffs who never gave him a fair shake at a decent part in a movie couldn't see him now. He had the Father Flanagan routine down pat and, lucky for him, most of the passengers on this cruise were old enough to remember Spencer Tracy in that role in *Boys Town*. He'd spent enough time on his knees serving as altar boy for the real Father Patrick Connelly, late of St. Mienrad's School for Boys in Omaha, so that the part came naturally. And what he didn't know he could always fake. But he was careful not to take it too far. He'd fallen about as far away from the church as he could go, but there were taboos even he wouldn't break. Like performing the Sacraments. If anyone asked, he lowered his head and let his voice get rough and low, and said, reluctantly as hell, that he was on sabbatical from St. Mienrad's because of a crisis of faith after the deaths of three of his favorite students in a car wreck. He'd come up with that little gem when a couple of rich old coots he'd been playing had asked if he would perform Mass since there was no other priest on board that sailing. They'd been gullible enough to swallow his story whole. And the "donation" they'd slipped into his jacket pocket the last night of the cruise "for the boys back at St. Mienrad's" had been the biggest score of the summer.

Looking like Spencer Tracy's clone didn't hurt any with the ladies, either, although he had to watch his step on this cruise. Word had trickled down from above through his partner, First Officer Giorgio Tzekas, that one or two passengers had been disturbed enough at his wining and dining a certain grass widow on the last cruise to complain to the staff. That's why he was making certain his quarry for this one, Myra Sandler, was always accompanied by one of her gaggle of daughters. On this cruise, he was on his best behavior.

Especially with the Boss on his case over the broken Greek urn. Damn that woman. She was a real harpy. It was just rotten bad luck the premier piece in his little collection was the one a careless steward had broken. Could have happened to anyone.

But the Boss wasn't just anyone. She was as tough and ruthless as any of the *camorra,* the Naples version of the Mafia that he'd been dealing with on and off the past ten years, ever since he gave up his going-nowhere acting career and took up a life of genteel crime as an art thief. The business suited him, or at least, it had until he took up with Tzekas and the mysterious woman he called Megaera, one of the Furies of Greek mythology, and who Mike usually referred to as the Boss. He'd never met her, never seen her face, only spoken with her on a phone that he suspected was designed to electronically alter her voice enough that he wouldn't recognize her even if they were talking face to face.

Not that he had any desire to be that close to the harpy. She was a real ball-breaker. Since the little gem of an urn had shattered into pieces on the floor of the ship's library, he'd had the nasty image in his mind of his own head in just about the same shape from a bullet in the brain. Tzekas was a greedy screw-up, and Mike suspected he gambled way more than he could afford. Weaknesses like that could get you killed dealing with the *camorra.*

He wanted out. And he'd been working on a plan to do just that. But, first, he needed a nest egg, small and portable and not too hard to get on and off the ship. The urn had been his first choice. The other genuine antiquities in his collection, the bust of Aphrodite, two Etruscan bronze disks and the Greek warrior frieze, were either too heavy or too big to risk getting through customs. His best bet now was a small Albanian icon. A triptych, older than dirt and worth a bundle on the antiquities black market. He could set himself up in style in the Caribbean for the rest of his life, if he could pull off the theft.

The triptych wasn't on board *Alexandra's Dream,* though. It was in a chapel in Rome, their next port of call, guarded by nothing more than half a dozen geriatric monks in a chapel that not only lacked any security but wasn't even wired for electricity. Technically, it would be a breeze to lift. Child's play, really. Except for one very important detail. The monk's chapel was located smack in the middle of the Vatican.

He wasn't a fool, nor an idiot. He knew there was no way he could get in and out of one of the Vatican museums, whose security rivaled that of Fort Knox. But the inconspicuous chapel of the Albanian monks, a refuge provided for them long ago and pretty much forgotten ever since, wasn't part of the system. No *Mission Impossible*-type heist for him. He was a small-town kind of guy, with small-town ideas. But that's what it took sometimes to outsmart the best security systems in the world: Faith and hard work and just a little bit of Irish luck.

He narrowed his eyes, momentarily diverted from his thoughts as he watched Myra Sandler dancing with one of the ship's gentleman hosts, Antonio Mendoza. This wasn't the first time he'd seen them together. There were rules governing the paid hosts on the ship. No more than two dances at a session with the same woman. Mendoza was on board to charm all the rich old gals, not monopolize one. Mike had put a word in the social hostess's ear. She had a soft spot for him. Her brother was a priest. The damned Spaniard had his choice of women. Mike didn't need the one he had chosen to relieve of some of her money.

He continued to watch as Mendoza escorted Myra back to her table. The youngest daughter, the one with the quick, sharp eyes and kissable mouth, gave her older sister a sideways glance that told him she wasn't certain what to make of Mendoza's marked attention to her mother. Good. He'd work on that mistrust.

He took a last swallow of his drink, dropped a dollar on the bar for the young Filipino bartender and exited the elegant, dimly lit lounge. He'd change his clothes and head for the observation deck where he knew Myra liked to spend a few quiet moments before retiring. It was another small boon to him that this sailing involved a day at sea so early into the cruise. It gave him more opportunity to sweet-talk the widow. Two days in Rome to work his magic and, by the time the ship sailed for the island of Corsica, their next port of call, he would have the triptych safely stowed in his cabin, his retirement secure and Myra Sandler one step closer to being charmed out of a hefty donation for "his boys." Perhaps, if all the stars lined up his way, he'd get something more—a night or two of forbidden love.

"THANK YOU, ANTONIO. I had a wonderful time. You dance like a dream. Please, won't you join us for a drink?"

"I would love to, *mi amor,* but I am afraid I have already broken the cardinal rule of a gentleman host. I have danced with you three times. That is not permitted."

"We're not dancing now," Myra pointed out. "We're sharing a glass of wine. My treat." She signaled to a waiter. "Oh, dear. They're all busy. Let's go to the bar."

Antonio gave her a soulful look and then a slow smile. "How can I resist? For you I would brave worse things than the wrath of the social hostess." He held out his hand.

Diamonds winked on her plump fingers as Myra put her hand in his and stood up. Light from the muted overhead fixtures sparkled in the gold and silver threads of her dress. Her mother was dressed to the nines tonight and, Lola had to admit, she looked great, her skin still smooth and her hair dressed by one of the stylists in the Jasmine Spa earlier that afternoon.

"Can I send you over a glass of wine, girls?" she asked, slipping her arm through Señor Mendoza's. She shot her daughters a dark look that told Lola she had seen her eye rolling and wasn't pleased with her behavior.

"Thanks, Mom, I'm good," Fran said.

"No, thanks. I'm drinking beer." Lola felt a little tickle of chagrin but shrugged it off. Myra had turned into the ship's social butterfly and Lola wasn't sure she liked it. First the priest, who had been hanging around all day. And now the gentleman host, or whatever you called it, Antonio Carlos Mendoza y Ortega, a Spaniard with ties to a major sherry-producing family—or so he claimed.

"Oh, good heavens," Lola muttered under her breath as the older couple walked away. "Can you believe the man? He sounds like one of those stick-up-the-butt English lords in the Regency romances Grandma Hilver always used to read. Remember? The simpering little misses looking for husbands on the Marriage Mart couldn't dance more than twice with one guy or they'd be *ruined*."

"Shh," Frances said, but the corners of her mouth twitched. "Yes, I remember those books, and he's nothing like that."

"He is so. No one talks like that, anymore."

"In the first place, he's Spanish and at least seventy. So maybe he does talk like that. And I kind of like him."

"He looks like a gigolo to me," Lola said stubbornly.

"Honey, for the last year and a half every man has looked like a gigolo to you."

"Not every man," Lola mumbled into her beer. For some reason the dark, rough-edged features of the ship's golf pro popped unbidden, and unwelcome, into her mind.

"Every man," Fran repeated.

The rebuke was gently spoken but hurt nonetheless because Fran was right. The worst thing about her marriage failing was the self-doubt it had left her with. She'd never been comfortable dating and playing the field. When she had let herself fall in love he'd turned out to be a loser. And a cad. Now she not only didn't trust the promptings of her heart, she didn't trust men period.

Lola looked up, refusing to let herself slip into a dark mood. "You got over your marriage failing. You date. I even thought you might marry that junior college prof you were seeing last year, what was his name? Tyrone?"

"We weren't right for each other. He wanted children, and, well, I already have two and that's enough for me."

Fran's face was as calm and placid as ever, but beneath the pleasant facade Lola sensed the hurt. "I'm sorry, sis."

"Don't be. It probably wouldn't have worked out. I'm too involved with my work, my kids—"

"Gary?"

Fran refused to be drawn. "Yes, even Gary." She

laughed a little and stood up from the small table where they'd been sitting with Myra. "Ex-husbands. Can't live with them. Can't live without them."

"Heavens, don't say that." Lola stood, too.

"I'm going down to the cabin to check on Bonnie." Their sister had excused herself after they'd left the ship's theater an hour earlier, saying she was tired and, since she couldn't drink, there was no use sitting in a nightclub, even one as elegant and understated as La Belle Epoque.

"All right. I'll tell Mom. Where is she?"

"There." Fran pointed to a small knot of people at the edge of the dance floor. Myra, her smile as glittery as her dress, was the center of attention. Antonio Mendoza was still at her side but the other men in the group were decidedly younger. At least younger than Señor Mendoza. Outside of a few singles and young families, Lola guessed the median age of the passengers aboard *Alexandra's Dream* to be somewhere in the midfifties.

"Good grief. Now look at her." Lola marched over to her mother. "It's getting late, Mom. I'll walk you to your cabin."

"Don't be silly, Lola. It's much too early to go to bed. Where's Fran?"

"She went to check on Bonnie."

"She's not feeling well again?"

Lola was tempted to say yes, that they needed to check on her, too, but couldn't bring herself to tell Myra such a worrying lie. "She's probably fine. I was hoping Fran could coax her on deck for some fresh air."

"Maybe she can. I'd like some fresh air, myself." Myra dimpled a smile at Señor Mendoza.

He smiled back and put his hand on his heart. "Alas, I cannot leave this room until the clock strikes midnight. It is my duty to see that all the other lovely ladies are partnered if they wish to dance, although, none of them will be as pleasurable to dance with as you."

Myra gave him a big smile and patted his arm. "How sweet of you to say so, Antonio. But, of course, you must stay and do your duty. I'll see you tomorrow for my lesson."

"Tomorrow we will tango. The dance of love."

Myra actually giggled. "I can't wait."

Lola ground her teeth, but she had to admit the man looked good in his tuxedo, his white hair smoothed back from his high forehead, his smile bright against his olive skin. "Good night, Señor Mendoza," she said pointedly, and, putting a hand to the small of her mother's back, hustled her out of the nightclub.

They entered the elevators and rode to the upper decks in silence. Myra still held her tongue as they stepped out on deck and walked to the rail, but Lola knew from a lifetime of experience that her mother had something to say. The salt air was warm after the artificial chill of the air-conditioned nightclub. It felt good against Lola's skin, silky and moist. She lifted her hair off the nape of her neck and let the breeze caress her skin as she watched white-tipped waves slide past far below.

After a moment her mother turned to her and said, "I'm disappointed in the way you acted in there tonight. Antonio is a nice man. I enjoy his company. You embarrassed me being so rude."

"I'm sorry, Mom," was all she could think of to say and knew it wasn't enough. "I guess I can't get used to seeing you with other men. It throws me off balance."

Myra was silent for a short time, then laid her hand on Lola's. "I have to admit I'm a little off balance, myself. Your father and I were together over forty years. I never looked at another man when he was living. And I haven't since he died. But I don't know. There's something about this trip, about this ship, that makes me realize I'm still really and truly alive and that I have a lot of living to do. I don't know how else to explain it. Don't you feel it, too?"

"I wish I could say I did," Lola said, smiling back.

"I've been worried about you since the divorce, Lola. Are you seeing anyone? Are you looking to your own future? I want you to be happy. To have a husband and family that make you as happy as I was with your father."

"I'm always looking to the future." Although Lola kept smiling at her mother, she felt a dart of pain pierce her heart. She could have left it at that but her mother was right. There was something about this ship, this cruise, that altered things, made it easier to say what was on your mind. "Maybe that's part of my problem. I can't enjoy the here and now because I'm worried about how it will be in the future." Reality returned with a rush as she heard herself speak the words. She laughed in embarrassment and waved her hand in the air. "Listen to me. I sound like one of those radio psychologists. That's all the self-analysis I intend to indulge in tonight." She touched the back of Myra's hand where it lay beside hers on the teak railing. "I'm sorry I embarrassed you in front of Señor Mendoza. I promise to behave from now on. Forgiven?"

"Forgiven." Myra gave her hand a squeeze and her smile turned impish. "But don't do it again."

"Scout's honor. I'll try my best." She put her arm

through her mother's and moved away from the rail. She could smell Myra's perfume, Estée Lauder's White Linen, the scent she'd worn as long as Lola could remember. "Let's go up to the observation deck. The stars are incredible, but there's too much light here to do them justice."

Myra held back a moment. She titled her head to look up into Lola's eyes. "You're so like your father. He tended to overthink everything, to weigh each and every detail of every decision he made. Always play by the rules, never any exceptions. It made him a good accountant, a good businessman. Sometimes not quite so good a human being. Do you understand what I'm saying, Lola?"

"Yes, Mom. All work and no play makes Lola a dull girl, right?" She tried for a light note and almost pulled it off.

Myra caught the slight break in her words and evidently decided she'd made her point. "Something like that," she said. "Honey, I'm not going to go off the deep end and run off to spend your inheritance on a gigolo half my age. I'm not even planning on doing that with one who isn't half my age. Come on, smile, Lola Roly-Pola. I promise no more scolding. Just pass the word on to your sisters to lighten up, and I'll forgive and forget. Deal?" She gave Lola's arm a squeeze.

Lola laughed. "Deal."

"Good. Perhaps we should go back down and check on Bonnie? She didn't seem quite herself to me tonight. Are you sure everything's all right with the baby?"

"She's fine," Lola sidestepped the issue. "Bonnie won't appreciate us hovering, and Fran is with her. They're probably watching *Under the Tuscan Sun*—it's playing on the ship's channel tonight."

"I suppose you're right, but still—"

"Tomorrow and the next day we're in Rome. Bonnie will be able to shop until she drops. That will perk her up." Bonnie didn't want Myra to know she was having doubts about carrying the baby to term. It would break the older woman's heart, and ruin the cruise for all of them.

"She did do a lovely job picking out that outfit for you in the boutique this afternoon. Thanks for going along with her." Myra gave the silky black jumpsuit and sheer, silver-embroidered, belted tunic-length jacket Lola was wearing an approving glance.

"Hey, it wasn't a hardship. Although, it was pricey." Lola smoothed her hand over the softly draping fabric. She liked pretty clothes. She just didn't have much call to wear them.

"It's just that I so seldom get the chance to see you dressed up."

"I'm a sports writer, Mom. I don't dress up. Ever."

"See. You just made my point again." They had separated to climb a wide, teak-planked stairway to the sports deck, where a walkway led to the observation platform that looked down onto the prow of the ship. Lola had turned back to take her mother's hand up the last steps when Myra's gaze skimmed past her and she said, "Oh, look. There's Eric Lashman. Gracious, isn't he a big chunk of eye candy in that tux?"

"Mom!" But Myra was right. He was eye candy, his tie undone, white shirt open at the throat, the heavy fabric of the tux stretched across his broad shoulders and powerful thighs.

"Lola, what did we just discuss?" Myra hissed, smiling and waving at the tall South African. "Lighten up! Let's go say hello."

Lola turned reluctantly. She wasn't ready to come face-to-face with Eric Lashman again, not until she was certain just what it was she wanted to learn about him. She'd e-mailed her boss back in Dayton that he was on board and that she hoped to get an interview with him. But she still hadn't figured out what direction that interview should take. Ethically, she shouldn't ask him any personal questions without identifying herself. She wasn't a tabloid reporter lurking in the bushes, handing out bribes to the gardener and pool boy, out to make big bucks or get her paper sued for libel. She had a week before the cruise ended. She intended to take it slow, step by step. Play by the rules. *Exactly as her father would have done.*

Or was her reasoning, and her hesitation, more complicated than that? Was she really only interested in the "where is he now?" aspect of his disappearance from the pro-golf tour? Or was there more to it? Was she just as interested in the man himself?

Eric Lashman did, indeed, look as if he'd stepped out of a fashion magazine. Except that he'd never be photographed by *GQ* doing what he was doing at the moment, practicing approach shots with a ten- or eleven-year-old kid on the putting green and, despite the tuxedo, seeming right at home doing it. Did he have any idea how sexy he looked dressed that way? How appealing it was when he reached down and gave the little boy a pat on the back and the kid looked up at the tall South African with a grin that nearly split his face in two?

"C'mon, let's stop and say hello," Myra urged. "You can apologize for missing the free lesson I signed you up for today."

She let that one pass. She'd told Myra she didn't

want a golf lesson from Eric Lashman, free or otherwise, but Myra hadn't listened. She'd "forgotten" it on purpose. But now it occurred to her that her mother had been right about one thing. She did overanalyze everything, including her personal relationships. Especially her personal relationships. She needed a little more spontaneity in her life. She needed a little more fun. She needed to stop treating every man she met as if he were her ex-husband.

She might as well start with Eric Lashman.

CHAPTER FIVE

"WAY TO GO, MATE." Eric tousled the kid's thatch of blond hair. The boy reminded him of Andrew at that age, all arms and legs and enthusiasm. He wasn't too bad a golfer, either. According to his ID tag his name was Tyler. He was eleven and had strayed from his group of ten- to twelve-year-old fellow cruisers, who were all girls and were forward on the observation deck watching the stars.

"Lame" was the way he described his evening, and who was Eric to tell him in another five or six years he wouldn't think stargazing with a group of pretty girls would be "lame" at all?

"This is so cool. I didn't know there would be someone to give me golf lessons on the cruise," Tyler said, lining up another putt.

There wasn't, technically. Eric's job was to give lessons to the adults on board, not to babysit their kids. But he figured it was better to keep the boy with him, in plain sight, until his handler discovered he was missing from the group and came looking for him. Of course, Eric could use his two-way radio to page whatever member of the crew was in charge of the ten- to twelve-year-olds tonight to have Tyler rounded up, but that would embarrass the kid so he hadn't done it. After all, there was only one way off the observation deck and that was right past where they were standing.

Tyler stroked another putt toward the flagstick but he pulled up on his swing and the shot bounced over the cup and rolled down the incline on the far side. It came up against the fiberglass netting that surrounded and canopied the putting green, saving passengers on the remainder of the sports deck from being beaned by an errant chip shot.

"Ease up, mate," Eric said, putting his hands on the boy's shoulders to straighten his stance. "Easy does it. Keep your head still. Think the ball through to the hole, then give it just enough of a push to make it over the rim."

Tyler lined up over his ball, straightened his shoulders, wiggled his hips and leaned into the stroke. His follow-through was good and the ball rolled to within six inches of the cup.

"Good shot," Eric said approvingly. He dropped another ball onto the turf. "Now, once more, slow and steady, and you'll have it."

Tyler pulled his lower lip between his teeth, gripped the club as Eric had showed him and gave the ball a firm push. It rolled to the hole, teetered on the lip of the cup and then dropped inside. "All right!" the boy crowed as though he'd just led a battalion of commandos safely through enemy territory. "I did it." He raised the putter over his head and shook it like a war club. "Tiger Woods, look out, here I come."

Eric didn't point out that Tiger would probably have broken every record there was and be making yet more millions on the Senior Tour by the time Tyler was old enough to go to Q school—the series of qualifying rounds an aspiring PGA golfer needed to win to join the tour. But he was no fortune-teller. Maybe someday he could say he knew the kid way back when. Was that what Andrew liked about being a teaching pro? Maybe he should give it another shot, himself.

No way. The denial came as quickly as the thought itself. He wasn't a teacher, didn't have what it took to do it day in and day out. What he wanted to do was to design golf courses, not teach. And not tour again.

"Nice shot, young man."

Eric looked around to see Myra Sandler and her youngest daughter approaching. They both wore black with touches of gold and silver, although there was no comparing the mother's black sheath and hip-length jacket with the sleek black jumpsuit and sheer embroidered tunic Lola was wearing.

"Thanks," Tyler said. "Mr. Lashman's giving me a lesson."

Myra nodded approvingly. "He's an excellent golfer. Take what he says to heart. I think with his help I should be able to shave a stroke off my handicap by the time I get home to Florida."

Eric didn't doubt what she said. Even from the short courtesy lesson he'd given her earlier, he could tell she was a good golfer with rock-solid fundamentals and a strong swing for a woman her age. He was looking forward to having her join him on one of the cruise outings, although she hadn't signed up for either of the Rome courses they were going to visit. She said her daughters would be scandalized if she chose a round of golf over the Eternal City, even if the course included an authentic Roman aqueduct.

"You golf?" Tyler asked, letting his surprise get the better of his manners. "You're as old as my grandma—" He realized what he was about to say and stumbled to a halt. "I mean—"

Myra laughed. "I know what you mean. And, yes, I expect I am as old as your grandma. I have three granddaughters around your age and two grandsons even older than that."

"Wow! You do? And you still like to golf? My grandma won't even golf with my grandpa if he takes a cart. She says it's too hard on her arthritis. But my grandpa says her arthritis doesn't seem to bother her when she spends all day at the mall."

"Why don't you show us another shot?" Myra broke in smoothly before Tyler spilled any more family secrets.

"Okay. Here's how Eric showed me to line up my putt." Myra stepped closer, careful to stay off the artificial surface with her high heels, and gave her full attention to Tyler's effort.

Eric looked over to see Lola watching him.

"How did you get stuck babysitting?" she asked. "I don't remember reading anything about junior golf lessons in the ship's brochure. Especially not at this time of night." Her voice was low pitched enough not to carry to the boy.

"He took off from his group. It's all girls tonight apparently and he couldn't take it anymore. If one of the kids' crew handlers doesn't show up in a minute or two,

I'll page them." He patted the pocket of his tux. "Didn't want to embarrass the kid by ratting him out the minute he walked up to the green."

Lola tucked her hands in the pockets of her silky jumpsuit, pulling it tight across her lower abdomen, defining the slight feminine rounding at the juncture of her thighs and causing his lower body to tighten slightly in response. An eddy of night breeze brought the scent of her perfume to his nostrils, something flowery and light, but with a more complicated undertone of citrus and spice.

"A guy thing, huh?" she asked with a smile.

He swallowed hard and hoped she didn't notice. "You could say so. We're mates now. Besides, I like kids."

"I do, too," she said. "Do you have any of your own?"

Did she? he wondered, but she didn't volunteer the information. He'd like kids of his own someday, a boy to teach to fish and play basketball and fix things around the house. And a little girl to cuddle and spoil. He'd like kids, but would he be better at being a father than his old man? He hoped so.

"No kids," he said. "Never been married. But I have a new niece. Karina. She's three weeks old, and only as big as my hand." He held out his hand and looked down at his palm, marveling as he did every time he thought of Andrew's daughter at how small she was. "She's a premie. But doing very well. That's why I'm on board. Filling in for my brother so he can be with his family."

"Congratulations. I have three nieces and three nephews." She let the sentence trail off as though she had meant to say more, but didn't, instead, turning her attention to Tyler, who was lining up his putt.

"Do you have children?" he asked. She didn't wear a wedding ring, but that didn't mean she wasn't married.

She swung her gaze back to his, her expression less open than it had been moments ago.

"No," she said, "I don't. Since my marriage lasted . less than two years, I guess it's good that we didn't have any." She returned her attention to the boy.

Uh-oh. Bad relationship. And she obviously wasn't over it yet. If he had the sense God gave a duck he'd back off, but he evidently didn't, because he intended to stay right where he was, close enough to reach out and touch her.

"Okay, Eric. Watch." The boy's voice gave him an excuse to look away from her green eyes.

"Steady on, mate," he said, shoving his hands in his pants' pockets so they wouldn't stray and reach out to touch the blond curls behind her ears.

Tyler adjusted his stance, and just as he was ready to take a stroke, a female voice intruded. "Tyler! There you are."

Tyler shanked the putt and the ball ricocheted off the screen and bounced around the green. He muttered under his breath.

Eric turned to see Gemma Slater approaching with four preadolescent girls in tow. The girls were all dressed in swingy sundresses, ribbons and sparkly combs in their hair, polished toenails peeping out of their sandals, giggles and smiles hidden behind their hands as they advanced on the outnumbered males. "You know you're not supposed to leave the group without permission."

"I got tired of looking at the stars," Tyler said, glaring at the quartet of girls with a look that signified more clearly than words that it wasn't the stars he was tired of. "So I came back to the kids' center to wait for you, and Mr. Lashman came over and offered to give me a putting lesson."

"How nice of him. But you still shouldn't have left the group without asking." Gemma pressed her hand to her heart and gave a rueful little smile. "You gave me such a scare. I was afraid you might have tumbled overboard."

"It wasn't that dark out there," he responded gruffly, but the tense set of Tyler's shoulders relaxed a little as he realized he wasn't going to be scolded in front of the Sandlers, and especially not in front of the girls. "I'm sorry. I forgot." He scuffed the toe of his shoe on the artificial surface of the green.

"That's okay. Just, please, remember to ask next time you want to leave the group."

"I will."

"So you've been having a lesson with Mr. Lashman?" Gemma's expression conveyed her gratitude to Eric for looking after her wayward charge. Gemma was the granddaughter of Elias Stamos, the owner of the cruise line. She was a tall, pretty girl of seventeen, with sun-streaked blond hair and dark eyes. She was working at the children's center on the ship during her summer school break in preparation for a career in early childhood development. Eric had met her once or twice at various meetings of the entertainment staff.

"Tyler's got a good eye and a steady swing," Eric said, smiling in return. "He's a natural."

"Perhaps we can come up here and you can help me with my putting tomorrow before we dock," Gemma said to Tyler. "The girls are going to have a spa experience with my partner, Monique, but I knew you wouldn't want to do that." She tilted her head slightly. "I'm correct about that, aren't I?"

Tyler swallowed and nodded so hard his ears wiggled. "No way," he said fervently. "A spa experience? Like where my mom goes? Yuck."

Gemma laughed gaily, as though he was the most clever male on earth, and Tyler's grin grew to twice the size. "I thought so. I promise tomorrow it will be just you and me. Is it a deal?"

"Deal," Tyler said, still grinning.

"Now, tell Mr. Lashman and the ladies good evening. It's time for us to go back to the rendezvous point and meet your parents." Gemma was a very pretty girl. She would mature into a stunning woman and it would be hard for any man between eight and eighty to resist her charm.

"Good night," Tyler said, including them all. He was now totally under Gemma's spell.

The quartet of girls smiled and giggled and murmured their farewells.

"Good night," Lola and Myra replied.

"In half a dozen years he will look back on this night and wish he could recreate it," Father Connelly said. The priest had breasted the stairway as the children began to descend and now stood aside to let them pass. "Good evening, all," he said, joining them on the edge of the putting green.

"Good evening, Father." The priest wasn't wearing his collar but dark slacks and a charcoal-gray turtleneck. Even in the Mediterranean in summer, the night was cool when you were moving at twelve knots.

"Father, what are you doing up here?" Myra asked.

"I came up to look at the stars." He lifted one eyebrow as he took in the putter and the golf balls scattered over the putting green. "And you?"

"I was hoping to do the same, but Lola and I were very enjoyably sidetracked by Eric and his young charge."

"Then would you ladies—" the priest indicated Lola in his invitation "—care to join me on the observation deck? I'd be happy to point out the unfamiliar constellations."

"I'd love to," Myra said. "What about you, Lola?"

Eric wasn't certain but he thought he detected a hint of a challenge in her words.

"Thanks, Father, but I think I'll pass. I'm going to call it a night. Tomorrow is a big day and I want to be rested." Lola's expression was polite but her eyes sparkled with their own hint of a challenge as she switched her attention to her mother. "Don't be too late, Mom. Bonnie's promised to shop till we all drop, remember?"

"I remember, and I'll be sure to get my beauty sleep." She handed the putter she'd been holding since Tyler left to Eric. "You handled the boy very well," she complimented. She tilted her head slightly and gave him a quick smile. "And since it isn't so very late, I believe you still owe my daughter a golf lesson."

"That was pretty obvious," Lola said as she and Eric watched her mother and the priest disappear into the shadows at the far end of the sports deck.

"Maybe she just wants her money's worth," Eric replied with a grin. "The lessons are expensive so you shouldn't waste the freebie, and technically there's still an hour and a half left in the day. Want to bone up on your putting since we're out here? Or do you want me to fire up the simulator?" He handed her Tyler's club and nodded toward the wraparound windows of the exercise room behind them, where three screens of sports programs kept the few diehard fitness buffs company. "It's state-of-the-art. You can play against Tiger at Pebble Beach, or take on Ernie Els at St. Andrews."

"Both of which you've actually done," she said, slipping the putter into the bag leaning against the netting.

"I have," he agreed. "But it was a long time ago. I take it that's a no, then, on the simulator?"

"You're correct." She grinned, but it took some effort. If she said yes to the lesson, he would want to watch her swing. Then he would want to give her pointers on improving it. And that would mean he'd come in close behind her, put his arms around her... She took a half step backward. She'd had golf lessons before, but never with a man like Eric Lashman. She would be close enough to smell his aftershave, feel the warmth of his skin, the hardness of his body. "It's a no," she repeated firmly. She didn't want to have those kinds of feelings again, woman's feelings, sexual feelings. Not now. Not yet. "I'm truly not interested in lessons. Golf takes too much concentration, too much finesse. It's too much of a head game for me. My mother knows that. She shouldn't have insisted on putting my name on your list."

"But she did and I have an obligation to see each passenger on that list gets their free lesson. How about hitting a few shots off the fantail, then? I guarantee you will never hit a drive as far again in your entire life."

"What are you talking about?" She had only been half paying attention to what he was saying. Mostly she was just listening. His accent was unique, unfamiliar, somewhere between British and Australian. Neither of those, she scolded herself. *South African.* Exotic to ears attuned to flat Midwestern twang and Appalachian drawls. And not only exotic, sexy as the devil. She could listen to him all day. Or all night. Images of Eric Lashman's pillow talk slipped through her thoughts and pooled low and deep in her stomach. Once more, her thoughts had veered into the sexual realm with no conscious prompting from her brain.

"C'mon, I'll show you." His words thankfully short-circuited her train of thought. He shrugged out of his tux jacket and pulled a driver out of the bag, then unzipped a sleeve of biodegradable balls from the side compartment. He motioned toward the stern end of the ship. "We're pretty sheltered here, but if I tee one up, the wind will catch it about thirty yards out and it will land halfway to Barcelona. Want to give it a try?"

"No way," Lola said, holding out her arms as though warding off an attack. "I'm left-handed, remember. If I took a swing with that club I'd probably put the ball through a window, or porthole, or whatever or, even worse, I might end up smacking some poor innocent in the back of the head. You do it. You're the pro."

For just a moment his face darkened, the lines at the corners of his eyes deepening, his mouth going hard, but almost immediately his smile returned and he took up her challenge. A faint vestige of the hardness remained in his voice, though. "Okay, I will. Anything to please the paying guest." He bent down and placed the tee in the soft, artificial surface and balanced a ball on top. He stood up and curled his hands around the grip of the club.

Lola waited, watching him take his stance, legs spread, head down. He gave the club one little wiggle then swung it up and back, his body following the curve of the club. She found herself holding her breath through the heartbeat of stillness at the top of his swing, and then let her eyes follow the slow beginning of a descent that picked up speed, like a blade dropping, as his powerful body unwound. The driver hit the surface of the ball with a small thunderclap of sound and the white sphere sailed up and out, hung against the black sky for a moment and then disappeared far astern into the foaming wake behind the ship.

"Wow," Lola said, impressed. "You were right. How far did you hit it?"

"Halfway to the moon," Eric said with a laugh, and all the hardness was gone from his face and his voice. His grin was almost as big as Tyler's had been when she and Myra found the two of them. "Are you sure you don't want to try one? It's a hell of a rush."

She shook her head. "I'm not going to try and follow that act and make a fool of myself."

"There's no one else to see," he said, holding out a ball. She looked down. The golf ball looked small against his big palm. He closed his hand around it and it disappeared. She wondered with another sudden tightening of her stomach muscles what it would be like to have his big hand close around hers.

She shook her head again, annoyed that she so quickly equated his every move with sex. She hadn't been this attracted to a man since…Jack. That revelation was like a cold shower. Her blood cooled. "No. You hit it." She spoke quickly, stiffly, so that it sounded like a command.

Without another word he teed up the ball and settled into his stance. A second loud "thwack" of clubhead meeting the ball, a second fleeting blur of speed as the white sphere arced into the darkness of the Mediterranean night, and then there was only silence and the faint sounds of music from the disco one deck down.

"End of lesson. End of demonstration." Eric slid the driver back into the bag and placed it inside a locker a few feet away, closing it and spinning the combination lock. He turned back to Lola. "Can I escort you some-where?" His words were formal, his tone polite but dis-tant. She'd almost forgotten his job on board ship was as much host as golf professional.

"No," she said hastily. "I…I'm going back to my cabin. I can find my own way." He wiped his hands on a towel from a shelf near the locker and dropped it into a laundry trolley. She hurried to speak before she lost her nerve. "Before I leave I want to apologize for what I said a minute ago. I'm sorry I brought that up, about your being a pro." And she was.

He lifted one broad shoulder in a shrug. "Don't be," he said. "I am a pro. I'm just not a touring pro anymore. And I don't ever intend to be again."

She wanted to ask him why. What had happened that April day at Augusta? Why had he walked off the course and never played professionally again? If she asked, would he tell her?

"I have a lesson at 6:00 a.m.," he said, shoving his long-fingered hands in the pockets of his slacks. "But I have time for a nightcap. Would you care to join me?"

"No," she said, and then softened the refusal with a smile. "It's late. I'm getting up early tomorrow, too. If you're going to see everything Rome has to offer in two days, you have to get an early start. Maybe some other time." It would be unprofessional to sit with him, drink with him, talk of family and friends and prospects for the future if she didn't tell him she wanted to interview him. And, if she told him that, she was certain she'd never spend a moment alone with the man again.

CHAPTER SIX

"I THINK YOU DID EXACTLY the right thing," Fran said as they settled into the motor coach that had taken them from the docks of Civitavecchia, Rome's dreary and industrialized port, to the city center for their second day of sightseeing in Rome. "It would be unethical to spend time with Eric Lashman if you didn't tell him up front you wanted to interview him. You've never been that kind of trashy, tabloid reporter. You've always played by the rules."

"There's never been much fodder for tabloid reporting in the sports department of the *Sentinel*," Lola reminded her sister dryly. At least, there hadn't been until she left on her cruise. She wondered what was going on with the steroid scandal back in Dayton. Had it led any closer to her ex-husband? Had he really committed a crime? Or was he just willfully blind to any problems with his team, the way he'd been to any problems with their marriage? As much as she liked to imagine seeing Jack perp-walked into the county jail in handcuffs, trying to shield his face with his electric-blue Lady Hornets team jacket, in reality she hoped it never came to that. Jack was a bad husband but he wasn't into peddling performance-enhancing drugs to college girls, even if it meant winning a national championship. She wasn't that bad at picking men, was she?

Lola slumped down and put her knees against the seat ahead, covering her eyes with the brim of her straw hat. Her head ached. Probably because there were thunderstorms brewing in the distance. She'd always been weather sensitive. And as she'd learned yesterday, the smog, for which Rome was infamous, would only get worse as the temperature climbed, adding to her misery. Rome in August. Heat and humidity, air pollution and, today, thunderstorms in the forecast.

Whose idea had this marathon two-day schedule been, anyway? Frances's, of course. Yesterday it had been shopping with a capital S. Today it was Treasures of Rome: The Coliseum, the Trevi Fountain, the Vatican museums, St. Peter's Square, the Basilica and the Sistine Chapel. They'd used the motor coach provided by the cruise line for their morning tour, but once they reached the Vatican they were going to strike off on their own, with Father Connelly as their expert guide. Lola groaned out loud. Just what she needed, the overattentive priest and Frances sparring over arcane minutiae of the Vatican treasures.

Bonnie leaned around the seat she was sharing with Myra and peered at Lola. "Are you okay? Didn't overdo shopping yesterday, did you?"

"I'm fine. Are you okay?" Lola responded, pushing the hat brim up a little so she could see her sister's face.

Bonnie smiled. "I feel fine. The best I've felt since we got on the plane. There's nothing like a full day of shopping, followed by a heavenly meal and a Broadway revue, to chase away the blues."

"But you didn't buy all that much." Myra had insisted they each choose something from the myriad boutiques and high-end designer stores that clustered around the famous Spanish Steps, but mostly they had gawked at the insanely priced clothes and jewelry with names like Armani, Dolce & Gabbana, and Brioni, the men's clothier who had tailored the suits for every James Bond since Sean Connery.

After thoroughly examining the merchandise at half a dozen stores, Bonnie had ended up choosing tiny, beaded evening bags for each of her daughters, which she said she intended to put away until they were old enough to appreciate them, and a silk designer tie for Tad. As a reward for her patience, Lola had gotten to pick out a beautiful hand-carved toy for Alex at an out-of-the-way shop on a side street so narrow and crooked she felt as if she'd stepped back in time at least two hundred years. Fran went with Armani ties for her boys, Gavin and Dustin, and ended up buying one for Gary, too.

Lola hadn't wanted shoes with heels that had to be registered as deadly weapons, or a purse so small she'd have to choose between her cell phone and her car keys, but she had wanted gelato. And she got it; three different kinds at a little café at the foot of the Spanish Steps, which, Fran couldn't resist pointing out, had not only been designed by the French but built by them, too.

Now, exactly twenty-four hours later, hot and weary, she was once more craving gelato as the bus pulled to a stop on a busy street outside the Vatican walls and deposited them on the ancient cobblestones. Dark clouds rolled overhead and thunder rumbled off in the distance, but not even the prospect of being caught in the middle of St. Peter's Square in a thunderstorm could dampen the enthusiasm of the disembarking passengers, Lola included, once she caught a glimpse of the overpowering sight.

"Do you think it will be as marvelous as the pictures?" she asked Fran, tilting her head to study the golden dome of St. Peter's as it towered over the skyline, awe-inspiring even when wreathed with rain-heavy thunderclouds. "My Lord, it's so big. Seeing a video just doesn't prepare you for the size, does it?"

"No photograph can do it justice," Fran murmured, clutching her Vatican guidebook.

"Oh! Oh, my goodness. It's really St. Peter's." Bonnie lifted her eyes to follow their gazes and drew in a breath. "It's amazing. I have to get some good shots for Mrs. Kozwalski, my neighbor. She's always dreamed of seeing the Vatican."

"Yes. It's really St. Peter's," Fran and Lola answered in unison, exchanging a smile of satisfaction at the excitement in their sister's voice.

Bonnie waved her umbrella like a drum major's baton. "Let's go."

"Hold on—we're waiting for Mom," Fran told her, laughing. "Here she comes."

Lola brought her gaze back to earth in time to see Father Connelly escorting their mother down the last step from the bus to the ground. He had been his usual attentive self the day before, sitting patiently at first one street-side café after another, sipping iced coffees as they shopped, carrying parcels, remarking on lesser-known points of interest they might otherwise have missed. So far today he had been equally attentive, but Lola still didn't like him. At least he was an American, though, and not the silky-mannered Señor Mendoza. As she watched, Father Connelly held Myra's hand for a second longer than necessary, bent his shaggy white head closer to say something in her ear, then followed her to where they were standing, his easy, craggy smile nowhere in evidence.

"I have some bad news," Myra said, sounding disappointed. "Father just told me he won't be able to accompany us on our tour of the Vatican. He… Something personal has come up he must attend to."

"I'm sorry, ladies," he said, his face solemn, his words sounding sincere. He was dressed in a traditional black cassock and a black straw hat today, with the small backpack he carried wherever they went. His hand closed over the silver crucifix hanging from his neck. "I really do apologize. It can't be helped." He, too, glanced upward at the golden dome. "I'll see you back on the ship, Myra." He touched the brim of his hat with the tip of his finger and crossed the street, disappearing into the deep shadows at the base of the medieval wall that surrounded the Holy See, the skirts of his cassock blowing in the fitful, humid breeze.

"We've been stood up," Lola said, keeping her voice carefully neutral so that her mother wouldn't take offense.

"Indeed, it looks as though we have," Myra agreed, staring at the spot they'd last seen the priest.

"I was looking forward to having him show us around," Bonnie said. "He seemed enthusiastic, too. At least until we stopped at that open-air market for our lunch break. When he came back from speaking to that man behind the produce counter, he seemed distracted. Didn't you think so, Lola?"

"I didn't notice," Lola said truthfully.

"He knows so much about the Vatican museums I was counting on him to show us all the things we'd miss on our own," Fran said. "I suppose we can go with the group from the ship." She sounded doubtful, then reached into her shoulder bag, coming up with a Vatican tour guide that was at least an inch thick. "Or we can use this."

"There now," Myra beamed, "we don't need Father Connelly. We have Fran, our own amateur Vatican scholar."

Fran waved off the praise. "Don't be silly. Father Connelly studied here, remember? Two years at the Etruscan museum. His lecture yesterday morning before we docked was very informative."

"But today he's stood us up," Lola said inarguably. She pointed toward their fellow passengers as they clustered around the young guide provided by the ship. "I'm positive you know more than he does. Let's not wait for them. I've been looking forward the whole trip to seeing the Sistine Chapel."

"Do you think we'll see the Pope?" Bonnie asked hopefully. "Mrs. Kozwalski would be in raptures if I brought home a picture of His Holiness."

"The Pope is at his summer residence, Castel Gandolfo," Fran said. "He isn't expected to make any public appearances for the next several days." The other Sandlers stared at her openmouthed, then exchanged nods of satisfaction. "What? I checked on the Internet last night. The Pontiff's schedule is posted there."

"See," Lola laughed, feeling her excitement building as they waited for a break in traffic to cross the street. "I told you we don't need Father Connelly. Let's go."

CHAPTER SEVEN

MIKE O'CONNOR WALKED quickly along the narrow sidewalk at the base of the Vatican wall, black cassock flapping against his legs, his backpack hanging against his shoulder blade. It was hot and humid, hell wearing black, but there was no way he could be out of character here, not with eighty percent of the ship's passengers and a good portion of the crew roaming the city. He was headed for Porta Sant' Anna—St. Ann's Gate, the entrance into "downtown" Vatican City, as he liked to think of it—but veered away from the ancient wall as he neared St. Anne's Parish church. Across the street a number of delivery vans were lined up, waiting clearance to enter Vatican City. He walked alongside them until he found the one he wanted, opened the door and climbed in beside the driver.

"*Ciao,* Paulo." The man in the truck was about his own age, dark hair going to gray, muscle going to fat, a cigarette dangling from the side of his mouth.

"Uh. You're late." The driver spoke in English.

"No matter," Mike said, sliding open the narrow door between the cab and the refrigerated storage compart- ment of the truck. Cold air and an earthy scent tensed his nostrils. Cartons and cases and sacks of fresh fruits and vegetables filled the space, all of the best quality, all destined for the Vatican supermarket where the citizens of the 108-acre compound, the smallest country on earth, shopped for their dinners. "You're behind schedule, too, Paulo," he said, climbing into the back of the truck.

"I suppose it was a woman that held you up." This time the other man made no attempt to hide his snort of disdain.

"Four women, actually," Mike said, grinning as he jerked off the stiff white Roman collar and pulled the cassock over his head.

"Pfft. It's always women with you."

"And it's always the turn of a card or the roll of the dice with you, cousin." Mike's family was pure Black Irish, but his mother's sister, Aunt Kate, had met and fallen in love with an Italian POW when he was brought to Ohio to work in the ketchup factory where she was employed. They fell in love, and after the war she fol- lowed him back to Rome. Paulo was their only child. And a more worthless piece of humanity Mike had yet to meet, except maybe for First Officer Tzekas. It was hell having to work with screw-ups.

But inadequate as he was, Paulo had his uses.

Mike folded his clerical garments and put them inside the lightweight nylon backpack and pushed it under the seat. He pulled on a white smock that matched his companion's, grabbed a baseball cap hanging from a hook and put it on his head, covering as much of his white hair as possible. He wasn't going to make a stupid amateur's mistake by using a false mustache or a wig. The Swiss Guard was trained to look for things like that. He slid onto the passenger seat just as his cousin let out the clutch and the truck rolled forward.

Mike held out his hand. "Where's my ID?" he asked. You could buy a ticket to tour the Vatican gardens or the museums, but no one just strolled through the gate into the city-state and wandered around on their own. Security was everywhere. And it was thorough. Even dressed as a priest he would never have made it past the public venues on his own.

But your average curious tourist didn't have a cousin who worked for the Vatican greengrocer. A cousin with a full-blown gambling addiction, and markers held by some of Rome's less savory and more dangerous citizens.

"Where's my money?" Paulo returned, lighting another cigarette from the stub of the last. He folded his arms across his chest and waited. Behind them, impatient drivers began to honk their horns. The gaudily dressed Swiss Guard at the gate turned his head in their direction.

Okay, let him win this one, Mike thought. He pulled out a thick roll of Euros. It was all the ready cash he had. He'd be broke until the ship's next payday, but damn it, he didn't have much choice. The Boss was on his case about the broken amphora. She'd grudgingly accepted his explanation of a clumsy member of the cleaning staff dropping the urn, but she hadn't been happy about it. And Mike didn't need her throatily whispered and very detailed explanation of just what part of his anatomy would be forfeit if any more such accidents should occur to her property to know she meant business. And she would probably delight in carrying out the punishment with her own two hands.

He shuddered just thinking about it. And for another reason, as well. A piece of the broken pottery was missing. He knew because he'd spent hours in his small, cramped cabin belowdecks gluing it back together. It wasn't just a little piece, easily lost under a shelf or chair, but a large one. Someone had taken it before he'd arrived in the library to document the damage to the "reproduction" urn. And there had been only one other person besides the terrified Czech crewman in the room. Ariana Bennett, the librarian.

Why had she taken the pottery shard? If she had taken it—and his gut told him she had—Mike needed to find out. He'd put out a few feelers to people he knew in the black-market-antiquities business and he was beginning to get some interesting hints. Ariana, it turned out, was the daughter of Derek Bennett, a former museum curator from Philadelphia, who had died while being investigated by the FBI and Interpol for possible involvement in antiquities smuggling, himself. It was too much of a coincidence for his daughter to show up on the very ship where he, Mike O'Connor, alias Father Pat Connelly, was doing the same thing. She needed watching. And, if she was up to something, alerting the Boss would be an excellent peace offering.

"This is only half what you owe me," Paulo growled, jerking Mike's attention back to the business at hand. "It wasn't cheap talking Alberto into calling in sick today so we could use his ID. I should charge you more."

"No way, cousin. We had a deal. Half now. Half when I get back. I know how busy you are. I wouldn't want you forgetting to wait for me."

Paulo snorted. *"Bastardo,"* he said, but without rancor. "The ID badge is in the glove box. Get it on. We're next through the gate."

Mike opened the glove compartment of the truck and pulled out a plastic ID tag. The name on it was Alberto DiAngelo. Gray hair. About Mike's age. The nose was too big and the face too fleshy, but all in all not too bad a match, if you didn't look too close. And with the overcast day, the tinted windshield and the backup of trucks waiting to get inside the Holy See, he was hoping the guard at the service gate would be just a hair less vigilant than usual. The stoplight on Italian soil turned green and they rolled through the shadow of Porta Sant'Anna into the bustling downtown of the ancient city-state.

Ten minutes later they had pulled up behind the Vatican supermarket, across the narrow street from the Vatican printing offices. "This is where you'd better pray we don't get turned back," Paulo whispered, grinding his cigarette butt into the floor of the truck with his heel. "The guard here will make a more thorough check of our credentials than the Swiss Guards at the gate."

"Why?" Mike whispered back, feeling sweat break out in his armpits and the small of his back. He'd been congratulating himself on making it past the Swiss Guard, stone-cold professional soldiers despite their gaudy, operatic costumes and giant meat-cleaver halberds—part pike, part battle-ax mounted on six-foot handles.

"Black marketeers," Paulo explained. "They just revoked one of *L'Osservatore Romano*'s employees' citizenship for trading butter to a restaurant outside the gates for free meals." *L'Osservatore Romano* was the semiofficial Vatican newspaper, as every Catholic knew. "*The Annona,* the Vatican supermarket—" his Italian cousin indicated the building they were parked beside with a tilt of his head "—has the best prices in Rome. On everything. Food. Alcohol. Tobacco. There is always someone wanting to make a little extra money reselling it on the outside. It's harder to get inside this building than it is to visit the Pope's apartments." He shrugged. "Or so they say."

"I'm not after cheap butter," Mike growled.

"And I don't want to know what you are up to," Paulo shot back under his breath.

"Identification," a guard in the uniform of the Vatican police force, the *Vigilanza,* demanded.

Mike held out his ID badge for the bored guard to scrutinize, careful to place his thumb where the shadow would blur the details of the picture. He made himself breathe normally, act normally. After a few words with Paulo and a cursory glance at the lading bill, the man waved them through. When the truck stopped, Mike hopped out, his heart beating hard in his chest. So far, so good.

He hefted one of the cases of tomatoes that were packed just inside the back of the truck and lifted it onto his shoulder. He followed Paulo into the back of the *Annona* and deposited his burden where his cousin indicated. As he'd hoped, by their third trip the guard paid no more attention. This time when Paulo grabbed a case of bananas, Mike reached through the opening into the cab and pulled his backpack from under the seat.

"You have twenty minutes," Paulo snapped, his dark eyes betraying nervousness as Mike jumped down onto the cobblestone pavement.

"I'll be back in eighteen." Mike grinned as he swung the backpack over his shoulder and began walking uphill along the ancient street, keeping the bulk of the truck between him and the guard, now busy with the next truck in line. He crossed two more narrow streets, keeping to the shadows of the centuries-old buildings that used to be stables and foundries and now housed the day-to-day workings of the little nation. He walked quickly, but casually, toward a small grotto at the edge of the Vatican gardens.

He'd discovered the place on an earlier visit, a VIP tour of the inner workings of the city-state, made on the arm of a lovely Italian contessa with family connections to the Holy See. It was on that visit that he'd also come across the object that he'd come to think of as his ace in the hole, his retirement fund. A fifteenth-century Russian triptych, painted on wood and small enough to slip into his backpack. He'd worked out the plan then, made contact with his long-lost cousin, set all the wheels in motion. Unfortunately he'd gotten greedy, lifted a pair of diamond earrings from the contessa's bedroom, and had gotten caught at it. He'd had to make a fast exit from Rome and hightail it back to the States before he could lift the relic.

He'd put the plan on hold, but it had always been there at the back of his mind. He bided his time, continued to research the Vatican and its environs, kept in touch with his scapegrace cousin, but the time had never been quite right to act—until he hooked up with Giorgio Tzekas and the mysterious woman who bankrolled their antiquities smuggling operation. But it had been the destruction of the Greek vase in the ship's library that had been the impetus for him to act now, on this particular trip to Rome. He needed a nest egg, something to fall back on if he had to make a quick getaway from *Alexandra's Dream*. After today he would have that insurance policy.

The entrance to the grove of trees that housed the tiny grotto the contessa had showed him two years earlier lay ahead. He looked around. His luck still held. There was no one on the path ahead or behind him. He stepped off the graveled walk, pushed through the spreading branches of some kind of bush he couldn't identify and entered the stone grotto, no bigger than a guest bedroom in a typical American tract house. He pulled off the greengrocer's smock, reattached his white collar and pulled the cassock over his head. He slipped the silver cross from beneath his black shirt and laid it on his chest, clipping the ID badge so that it was partially obscured by the cross.

Then he slung his pack over his shoulder and strolled out into the stormy afternoon, admiring the plantings, the palms and magnolias and manicured flower beds, changed with the seasons to ensure they were always in bloom. His destination was a tiny stone chapel located off the main pathways frequented by the thousands of legitimate visitors to the gardens, so secluded it might have been forgotten by time itself.

His first visit to the chapel, which was screened by cypress trees, had been pure serendipity, blind luck. He kind of liked to think it was a minor miracle. Since that fateful day he'd learned everything he could about it, precious little though that was. The chapel had been given to a small order of Albanian monks hundreds of years ago by a Pope whose name had been drilled into Mike's schoolboy head by the real Father Pat and forgotten even more quickly. It was to be a refuge from the seemingly endless warfare in their Balkan homeland. Now, centuries later, a bare handful of monks, all that remained of their ancient order, still resided within its stone walls. When the last monk died, the chapel and its contents would revert to the Holy See. And sooner or later a librarian or curator or some other official from one of the museums would come to inventory the contents.

A gardener pushing a wheelbarrow piled high with cuttings crossed his path, nodded and hurried on, casting quick peeks at the darkening sky as he walked. Mike's heart picked up a couple of beats, then settled back down as the gardener paid him no attention. So far, so good. He had no illusions that he could make off with any of the Vatican's thousands of priceless treasures. Security was state of the art.

But the Albanian monks were a poor order. They could afford none of the technology that guarded the Church's most valuable treasures. It had been almost two years since Mike had set foot in the chapel, but he doubted anything inside had changed. The monks were old, they cared nothing for what went on outside their small sanctuary and the life of prayer and contemplation they embraced. Worldly wealth meant little to them. He wondered if they even knew how valuable the wooden triptych on the rough side altar was worth in dollars and cents. He suspected they didn't.

He walked quickly, a busy priest hurrying to his destination before the impending storm. But the gardener had passed him and there was no one else in sight. The chapel came into view as he turned onto a narrow pathway that curved around to the entrance. The carved wooden doors, dark with age, were open as he knew they would be. He stepped inside, waiting a moment to let his eyes adjust to the near darkness of the stone interior. The church was empty, the only light coming from candles burning on either side of the main altar. The air inside was cool compared to the humid afternoon outside, redolent with the scents of incense and dust and time itself.

Nothing had changed.

Mike smiled and walked quickly down the aisle between the narrow stone pews. Silence surrounded him. At this time of day the monks were at their prayers in the small adjoining dormitory where they lived, locked away in their stone cells, alone with their beads and their God. The chapel was unguarded, and the triptych he had come in search of would be unguarded, as well.

He turned left at the main altar, as plain and spartan as everything else in the building, and entered a tiny alcove where a single candle burned on either side of a stone table. And there it was. A triptych of the Holy Family with a haloed Infant Jesus in the middle. The colors were muddied with age, the style primitive, but Mike had no doubt what he was looking at. A fifteenth-century Russian icon, its distinctive style proclaiming its origin in the workshop of the tsars, given to the monks by Catherine the Great in gratitude for providing sanctuary to one of her cousins—or, more likely, her lovers—when he'd been set upon by bandits and nearly killed.

Later the monks had brought the triptych with them when they, in their turn, fled persecution. It had languished in its small alcove ever since. But not for much longer. When he was through with it, the triptych would have found its way into the private vault of some collector in America or Japan. It would be kept at optimum temperature and humidity and sealed away from harmful light and pollutants—and never seen again.

But that wasn't his problem. He unzipped the backpack, which held an exact reproduction of the triptych.

The contessa had thought him a little crazy to take so many pictures of an ugly wooden painting in such an out-of-the-way spot that day two years before. But she had humored him as he'd snapped half a dozen quick shots from various angles before being spotted and asked to leave by an outraged monk who looked to be ninety if he was a day. Later Mike had given those photos to the reclusive German artist whose forgeries were hanging in museums and private collections the world over, the man who had originally introduced him to Tzekas. Six weeks later Mike had the expertly aged reproduction in hand, identical in every detail to the original, thanks to his forger's talent and computer technology. He'd kept it with him ever since, waiting for this very moment.

The switch of the unguarded and unprotected icon was accomplished in a matter of seconds, the fake placed exactly in the faint dusty outline of the original. Mike remained kneeling before the coarse stone altar until he had his breathing under control once more, a pious priest at his devotions. Then, making the sign of the cross, he stood, smiled and headed for the entrance two minutes ahead of schedule, a full half hour before the geriatric monks would file back into the sanctuary for afternoon Mass.

Lightning arrowed down from the dark sky, thunder followed in its wake and the skies opened. Rain came down in torrents, and for the first time Mike felt a shiver of uneasiness scamper across his nerve endings. The backpack was waterproof. He wasn't worried about the triptych, but he didn't like thunderstorms, didn't like getting wet, and for all his life he'd been afraid of being struck by lightning. Not to mention the fact that he would prefer to avoid showing up at the *Annona* looking like a drowned rat.

He hesitated just inside the carved doors, wondering if one of the monks would break his meditation to come close them. Probably not. The doors were recessed into the stone wall, and the floor was also stone, as were the pews. What harm could a little rain do? He waited, impatient now, scowling out at the storm. Suddenly a figure raced up the chapel's stone steps and the gardener Mike had seen earlier skidded to a halt in front of him.

The man grabbed for his cap and ducked his head. "Excuse me, Father," he said in Italian. "I just wanted to take shelter from the rain."

"I'm sheltering from the rain, too," Mike replied in the same language. His Italian wasn't that good, but he could get by in day-to-day conversation.

"I don't think it will last long. August thunderstorms never do." The gardener looked out at the rain, which did seem to be letting up. That Mike was a foreigner didn't even warrant a second glance. The Vatican was full of people from different countries. Mike relaxed a little, leaning against the stone pillar that supported the chapel roof.

"I hope so," he said. "I'm late for an appointment." He took a quick glance at his watch. Thirteen minutes since he'd walked away from the back of the truck. If he didn't leave the church in a minute or two he would lose his bet with Paulo. It was a long shot, but his cousin just might get a burr up his butt and leave him behind as he'd threatened. Mike's pulse accelerated a couple of beats.

"The rain will cleanse the air," the gardener mused, nodding wisely. Even in the middle of the Vatican gardens, Mike's eyes stung from the smog that wrapped Rome in a haze of car exhaust and industrial fumes.

"God's will," Mike said, crossing himself. He hitched the pack higher on his shoulder.

"Are you really going out into the downpour, Father?" the gardener asked, settling against the opposite column, preparing to wait out the storm.

"I'm afraid I must." Mike moved away from the column and braced himself for the onslaught of the cold rain.

"Father, wait." The gardener reached out and laid his hand on the backpack.

Mike froze in his tracks. Surely the man couldn't tell what was hidden there, could he? The triptych wasn't much bigger than a notebook, and not particularly heavy.

"One moment, Father."

Mike turned, his expression showing nothing but innocent concern. He was a damned good actor even if he'd never made it big in Hollywood. "Yes, my son?"

The gardener bowed his head. "Your blessing, Father."

"Of course, my son." Mike let out a sigh, made the sign of the cross and mumbled a few words of Latin he remembered from his youthful days as an altar boy. "Peace be with you," he said, and headed down the chapel steps into the rain.

Four minutes later, dripping wet, he was back in the grotto. He hadn't had to worry about being seen this time. The rain had emptied the streets and walkways of the Vatican just as it would anywhere else. He folded his wet cassock and slid it into the outer pocket of the backpack and pulled on the grocer's smock once more. The rain had dwindled to sprinkles when he stepped back onto the street leading to the supermarket. Slowing his pace, he retraced his path, keeping the truck between him and the building. He reached the back and peered inside. It was empty. Paulo was probably delivering the last case or he would have shut the big double doors.

Mike pulled himself up onto the floor of the truck and waited. Thirty seconds later he heard his cousin's footfalls on the cobblestone pavement. Paulo walked with a very heavy step. Mike hopped down and shut the first of the doors as Paulo rounded the back of the truck.

"You're back," he said unnecessarily. He was as wet as Mike and wasn't happy about it.

"I told you I would be."

"Get in the cab," Paulo growled. "I want to get out of here and get some dry clothes. Did you get what you came for?" He gave Mike a sideways look as he put the truck in gear. Mike hadn't told his cousin any of the details of his quest, and Paulo was just as happy not to know—as long as he got his money.

"I did," Mike said, and turned his attention to the guard at the gate, who was huddled into the shelter of his overhanging eaves. One last hurdle and he would have pulled it off. He would have his nest egg, his passport to the life he wanted to live in his "golden years," and a fallback if the gig he was involved in went south, as his instincts were beginning to warn him it might. Mike had always trusted his instincts. For the most part they'd kept him out of jail, and gotten him out of more jams than he cared to remember. If his gut told him to watch out, he did.

Paulo idled the truck at the last checkpoint and handed over their authorization papers. The guard gave the papers and ID badges a cursory once-over, glanced at Mike's backpack on the floor, giving his heart one last painful jolt of adrenaline, then waved them through.

Unchallenged, they passed beneath the shadow of the Vatican walls back onto Italian soil. Mike pushed his hand through his short, white hair and grinned. "God-dammit," he said, and it was as much a prayer as a blasphemy. He had done it! Outsmarted Vatican security, the best on the planet, and made off with a valuable church relic. The robbery of the century—and no one would ever know. No one but him.

CHAPTER EIGHT

"MY FEET ARE KILLING ME," Myra complained as they moved out of St. Peter's into the crush of afternoon traffic surrounding the square. "My ankles are as big as elephant legs. I need to find a place to sit down."

"I'm tired, too," Bonnie seconded. "We've got an hour to kill before the bus comes, thanks to Fran being such an efficient tour guide."

The spell of the Vatican was wearing off as they left St. Peter's Square. The basso roar of idling tour buses, the blare of taxi horns and the high-pitched whine of motorbikes replaced the relative quiet of the Papal City. Lola did her best to hang on to the awe engendered by the immense size and grandeur of the basilica itself, the heartbreaking perfection of the Pieta, the glory of Michelangelo's Sistine ceiling and Last Judgment, but it was a losing battle amid the heat and humidity and her mother's increasingly numerous complaints.

"There must be somewhere in one of those guide-books where we can sit down and take a load off our feet," Myra prodded her oldest daughter.

Fran was already rummaging in her shoulder bag. She flipped through the pages then spent a few moments perusing a paragraph or two. She looked up, read a little more, then closed the book, keeping the place with her index finger. "That way," she said. "If the book's correct, this street is closed to traffic in a couple of blocks. A lot of people who do business with the Vatican live there. It's called the Borgo, and the book describes it as 'a wonderfully civilized neighborhood.' There are shops and restaurants and the souvenirs are cheaper than they are in St. Peter's Square."

"You're sure it's only a couple of blocks?" Myra began to fan herself with the museum brochure she was still holding.

"That's what the book says."

"Great, I can buy Mrs. Kozwalski a rosary," Bonnie said. "She's helping Tad's mom keep an eye on the kids, you know."

"Let's go," Lola said. "I could use something to drink. And it looks like it might storm again." She led the way into the maze of motorbikes and tiny Roman cars and got them all safely across the street and headed in the right direction.

Fifteen minutes later they were seated under an umbrella on the outdoor patio of an unpretentious sidewalk café, drinking lemonade, menaced by nothing more than the occasional moped and a gang of dark-haired, olive-skinned little boys playing soccer in the middle of the street.

"This is fantastic," Bonnie said, ignoring her lemonade in favor of framing street shots with her digital camera. And it was a lively scene. Small stores and shops spread out in both directions. Colorful umbrellas marked the restaurants and coffee shops, and crates of fruit and flowers overflowed onto the sidewalks in front of the retail stores. A tiny, wizened nun in a black habit and starched-white wimple, her skirts tucked under her, sailed by on a moped while clean laundry flapped on lines strung from window to window of apartments leaning close to each other above the narrow cobbled street. Bonnie laughed and snapped away, in her element.

"Let me see," Myra demanded, holding out her hand for the camera. Bonnie obliged and Myra bent her head to peruse the images on the small screen. "That's what I like about digital cameras. Instant gratification. These are lovely." Myra shielded the screen with her hand to keep out the glare of the sun as it attempted to break through the haze. "The storm clouds above the dome of St. Peter's give me goose bumps. And the one of Father Connelly is very flattering even if he didn't seem to want his picture taken. And I love this one of Lola eating gelato." Lola groaned. Bonnie had inherited her irritating tendency to snap unflattering photos of them eating from their mother. "But this one of me stuffing my face with that marvelous pastry we had yesterday has to go. I just love this little delete button. Makes all your mistakes go away like magic."

"No fair, Mom," Lola said, making a grab for the camera. "If you get to delete pictures of you eating, so do I."

"It's my camera," Bonnie reminded them both,

nimbly snagging the camera as Myra dangled it from the wrist strap. "I'm in sole charge of the delete button."

She turned in her seat, dialed up the video setting and began filming the comings and goings around them. A few seconds later she hit the off button and looked up from the screen. "Isn't that Father Connelly?" she asked, pointing back to where a line of delivery trucks rumbled in and out of the Vatican gate.

"Where?" Myra asked, setting her lemonade glass down on the iron table so hard it chimed a protest. "I don't see him."

"There," Bonnie said. "He's just getting out of that white truck. See, I recognized his white hair and that black straw hat he was wearing."

Lola and Frances turned to look. "That's him, all right, talking to the guy in the truck. My Italian's not very good but 'fresh fruits and vegetables' in four-foot-high letters isn't hard to translate. How odd."

"You're right, it is odd," Myra said, raising her carefully tweezed eyebrows. "He told me he was going to see an old friend of his who is still assigned to the Vatican. He said he needed to talk with him about the direction he was going to take in the future. He led me to believe he was having some personal doubts about remaining in the priesthood." Her voice sharpened slightly. "But he never said his friend was a deliveryman."

"Well, there's no law that says he can't be," Lola said, keeping her voice carefully neutral.

"Yeah, right," Fran agreed, but she wasn't as successful at keeping the doubt from her voice. While they'd been talking, Father Connelly had bid farewell to the cigarette-smoking man in the truck and disappeared between two idling tourist buses in the direction of St.

Peter's Square, where they were to meet their own bus in another half an hour. "I'm sure he's got a reason for it," she said, backtracking a little.

"I'm sure he does," Myra said briskly, but her frown had deepened.

Good, Lola thought. I hope she starts thinking twice about everything he tells her from now on. Not only had Myra come out of her shell on the cruise, she'd blossomed into *Alexandra's Dream*'s social butterfly. Of course, even with Father Connelly out of the way, Lola would still have Señor Mendoza to worry about. But she'd cross that bridge when she came to it.

"Here comes someone else we know," Bonnie said, abandoning a study of the soccer-playing children and the small brown dog that had interrupted their game in favor of another subject.

Lola glanced in the direction Bonnie was looking, and sucked in a breath. It wasn't the photogenic children Bonnie was taking pictures of, it was a man, and not just any man.

"Hello, Mr. Lashman," her sister cooed as he approached their table, giving him her familiar, contagious smile, a smile that had been too little in evidence before today.

"Hello," he said, bending his head to avoid being poked in the eye by the umbrella spokes. "And, please, call me Eric." He nodded greetings to Fran and Myra and turned his gray gaze on Lola. "Hello," he said in that whiskey-and-smoke voice that set her nerves atingle.

"Hi." The single-word greeting was all she could manage until she caught her breath.

"Have you ladies enjoyed your day in Rome?" he

asked politely. He was wearing the dark blue shirt and khaki slacks that all the sports staff aboard *Alexandra's Dream* wore, but on him it looked anything but uniform. His broad shoulders strained the cloth and the pants molded to his muscular thighs and firm butt as though they had been tailor made for him.

"Wonderful. The Vatican—" Myra waved her hands, the stones in her rings catching stray winks of sunlight "—it leaves me at a loss for words," she finished with a self-deprecating smile.

"I agree."

"You were sightseeing, too?" It wasn't unusual that they wouldn't have run into him on their tour. The Vatican museums were vast, as were the basilica and St. Peter's Square.

"My afternoon golf outing was canceled due to the weather. Liberty Line doesn't want its passengers getting struck by lightning on the course. I took the opportunity to do a little sightseeing on my own."

"And what did you think of the place?" Myra asked in a teasing voice.

"It leaves me speechless," he said, and grinned.

Myra, Fran and Bonnie laughed at his joke, Lola's laughter stuck in her throat, but she managed a smile.

"Won't you join us?" Fran asked.

"I don't want to intrude."

"You're not intruding," Bonnie insisted, beaming. "We're just soaking up the atmosphere until it's time to head back to the bus. What are your plans for the rest of the evening, Mr. Lashman? Eric," she corrected herself when he opened his mouth to object.

"I was planning on having dinner here in the city," he said, pulling up a chair from an empty table and wedging it between Bonnie and Myra. "There's a late train to Civitavecchia. We don't sail until midnight."

"That sounds nice," she said. "Fran, I need to buy a rosary for Mrs. Kozwalski, remember. Will you come with me?"

Fran looked up a little startled, as though she'd been pinched or kicked in the ankle under the table. Lola narrowed her eyes. Something was up.

"Mom—" Bonnie directed her next salvo at their mother "—didn't you say you needed a new pair of sunglasses? I'll bet they're a lot less expensive in one of these shops than they were where we shopped yesterday."

Myra's eyes widened as Bonnie plucked her lemonade glass out of her hand and picked up her purse, but she followed the cue. "Why, yes. I suppose I could use a pair of sunglasses. You'll excuse us, Eric, won't you?"

"Of course." He began to rise from his chair but Myra laid her hand on his shoulder. "We'll be back in twenty minutes, Lola," she said with a wave of her fingers, and just like that her mother and sisters marched off to do battle with the merchants of the Borgo, leaving Lola alone with Eric Lashman.

"That was even more obvious than her maneuver on the sports deck," Lola said, wishing she could drop through the pavement into the catacombs that were said to lie beneath this part of Rome.

"It wasn't subtle," he agreed, scratching the tip of his ear, "but I'd be an idiot not to take advantage of it. I'm free for the evening. Would you like to stay in the city and have dinner with me?"

Lola felt herself flush and hoped he didn't notice. She looked down at her coral-pink cotton shirt and midcalf denim skirt, appropriate attire for a Vatican visit but not a night on the town. He caught her hesitation and waved his hand to encompass the lively street scene surrounding them. "Nothing fancy. I planned to have dinner here. My brother told me about a great Thai restaurant just down the street."

"Thai?" It wasn't what she'd been expecting to hear him say.

He laughed. "We don't have to eat Thai. I love Italian, and where better to get it, I suppose?"

"That's more like it," she said. "I'd love to have dinner with you," she added before the warning whisper in the back of her head grew too loud to ignore.

"Fine. I'll start by buying you a glass of wine."

"Thank you." She was going to need some fortification to deal with her mother and sisters when they came back to collect her.

The waiter came, Eric gave him their order, in Italian, and he returned promptly with two glasses. They sat quietly sipping the crisp white wine and watching the world go by. As she watched, Lola felt the weight of the e-mail from her editor, a golf fanatic himself, in her skirt pocket, giving her the go-ahead on the interview. *Tell him now,* her inner voice prompted. *Get it out in the open. If he refuses an interview you have time to go back to the ship with your family, before you make a fool of yourself.*

"What did you like best about the Vatican?" he asked when the silence had begun to stretch out a little too long.

"The ceiling of the Sistine chapel," Lola replied gratefully. "The scope, the color, the genius—" she lifted her hands in defeat "—and the sheer guts and determination it took to paint it."

"I've been to Rome half a dozen times. I try to see it every trip if I can. But my favorite spot is in the Basilica, under the dome. Architecture is kind of a hobby of mine."

She wouldn't have guessed that about him. "Michelangelo designed the dome, too," she said. "I rented *The Agony and The Ecstasy* a couple of weeks before we sailed."

"Great flick." She hadn't expected him to be a fan of old movies. Her surprise must have shown on her face.

"My mother was an American. We lived in North Carolina for a couple of years until I was eight. After she died my dad wanted to go home." His voice hadn't changed but something in his eyes told her the sorrow of losing his mother was still there after all these years. "He moved us to Cape Town. It was in the middle of the sanctions. Not a great place to live at the time. Watching old movies and TV shows kept me and my brother from feeling homesick."

"And what's South Africa like now?"

"It's better. Things are improving and it's become a big tourist destination. I have a home there, but I still spend time in the States. I have cousins in North Carolina."

"You do?" Lola stopped herself before she added, "What does your home in Cape Town look like? Where do you live when you're in North Carolina? Are you seeing anyone on either continent?" She'd deliberately stayed out of the Internet café on the ship. She hadn't Googled his name a single time since the second day of the cruise. But she had to stop asking personal questions until she told him about herself.

"Can't picture me as a good ole boy?" he asked in a laid-on-thick-as-molasses Southern drawl.

Lola laughed. "Not with that accent."

He grinned. "Back in Cape Town people complain I sound like a Yank. If it proves my bona fides, I'm a NASCAR fan, how about you?"

She loved NASCAR racing. This was a perfect opportunity. She could say, "I love racing. I follow it in my work…" She opened her mouth and was immediately surrounded by her mother and sisters, who appeared out of nowhere, it seemed to Lola. Of course, if she hadn't been focused so intently on Eric Lashman's gray eyes, she might have seen them coming.

"We're heading back to the bus," Fran announced. "Mom's getting tired."

"I have a dinner engagement with Señor Mendoza," Myra said, gathering up the bags she'd left for Lola to watch. "I want to get off my feet so we can go dancing."

"And I just want to get off my feet, period," Bonnie seconded. She pushed her sunglasses down the bridge of her nose and looked at Lola over the tinted lenses. "You have a full glass of wine, I see. Want to meet us back on the bus after you finish it? We still have a few minutes."

"Actually, I'm having dinner with Eric," she said, staring at the gold stud in Bonnie's left ear. "We're taking the train back to the ship later."

"Great," her sister said without batting an eyelash. "We won't wait up for you. Goodbye, Eric." Bonnie gifted him with one more of her infectious smiles and shooed her mother and sister back onto the cobblestone street. "I'm going to call Tad and tell him everything that happened today. I don't care how much it costs."

Lola's mouth popped open. "She's calling Tad?" she mouthed to Fran.

Fran looked back over her shoulder and shrugged, but she was grinning. "I'll let you know," she mouthed back, and then they were gone, swallowed up by the traffic beyond the street barricades. The little boys, as well, had finished their game and melted into the comings and goings on the busy street; only the old men smoking and gossiping on their park bench were left. For a moment Lola and Eric were alone in a pool of relative quiet.

"Would you like another glass of wine?" Eric asked.

"What? No. No, thank you." Lola realized she was still staring into the distance even though she could no longer see her mother or sisters in the crowds milling around the tour buses.

"Is something wrong?" He was very intuitive—she'd noticed that about him the night on the sports deck. He watched people, studied them, not in a creepy way, but as though he were trying to figure out what made them tick, how to best deal with them.

"No. Not really." She picked up her glass and took a sip. "Family stuff," she said, knowing it wasn't much of an answer.

He nodded. "I understand." He was making circles on the filigreed iron tabletop with the bottom of his wineglass.

"It's complicated."

"Families usually are," he said, looking up at the same time she did. Their eyes met and held.

"My sister, Bonnie, is pregnant," she heard herself say.

"And she's not happy about it?"

He was good. "Yes. How did you know?"

"Just took a guess. She's what, in her late thirties? She doesn't strike me as the kind of woman who put her career in front of motherhood. So I'm thinking she already has children. And besides, I believe I overheard your mother say she had three granddaughters and two grandsons—"

"Three actually."

"Three grandsons. That's a total of six, and I remember, also, that you said you have no children. So…"

"So you figured one of my two sisters had more than the average 2.7 children."

"And that sister is Bonnie, correct?"

"Correct. This baby will be number five."

He whistled. "Supermom."

Lola smiled, cupping her empty wineglass between her hands. "She is, you know, a real supermom. And Tad, my brother-in-law, is a great dad. But this pregnancy was a big surprise and, well…" She looked down at her glass for a moment, swallowing the lump of worry that had risen in her throat. "She's…she's talking about not…not carrying the pregnancy to term."

"And you don't want her to take that step?"

"Theoretically, I'm not opposed," she said, incurably honest. "I know it's her choice. But she's my sister. The baby is my niece or nephew. And that makes all the difference in the world. I hate it when abstract concepts jump up and bite you in the butt."

He laughed, leaning back in his seat. "I'm sorry, I couldn't help myself. You have such a way with words."

Guilt shouldered her anxiety over Bonnie out of the way. Tell him now, her conscience goaded. It's the perfect opening. *Thanks. I'm really a sports reporter, you know, temporarily exiled to the Women's Page. Would you like to give me an interview?* That would probably send him running for the hills as fast as his long legs would carry him. He was an intensely private man—she could surmise that from how thoroughly he'd stayed out of the media spotlight for the last four years.

"Is her husband okay with her decision?" he asked, and Lola knew her window of opportunity had slammed shut.

"No, he isn't. They must have had a fight over it before we left for the cruise. That's another reason I've been worried about her. They've got a really tight marriage. This might ruin it for them."

"Do you think her saying she's going to call him is a good sign?"

She let her thoughts turn inward for a moment. She recalled the smile on Fran's face and remembered her own answering one. "Yes," she said, relaxing against the back of her chair. "I do."

"I'm glad. Babies are wonderful. I can't wait until my niece is big enough for me to spoil rotten." She remembered that, too, from their conversation on the sports deck. He liked children, and wanted a family of his own.

So did she, she realized suddenly. She hadn't let herself dwell on it, but one of the things that upset her most about her divorce was that her chance to have a baby anytime soon had died along with her marriage.

"Karina, I believe you said her name was. It's lovely." She could wait just a little longer to tell him the truth about herself.

"She's a sweetheart. I have pictures back on the ship. I'll show you sometime." Her heart did a little flip. Did that mean he wanted there to be "a next time"? Another dinner? Perhaps more?

Thunder rumbled from somewhere behind the dome of St. Peter's. "Uh, oh," he said, peering out from under the edge of the umbrella at the darkening sky. "Looks like the weather's turning on us again. It's a little early for dinner for the locals." He glanced at his watch.

His hands were big, long-fingered, and his wrists were strong and tan. Lola swallowed hard as she imagined what those hands would feel like against her skin. "Actually," he said, "it's a lot early. But there's a place another block or so along this street that my brother told me about. Strictly low-key, mostly locals. They serve good antipasto and *assaggini misti.*"

"What's that?" Lola asked as he laid some bills on the table for their wine.

"A pasta sampler," he said, teeth white against his tanned skin.

"Carbohydrate heaven," she said. "Right up my alley. Lead the way."

"What is your alley, by the way?" he asked, holding out his hand to help her up from the low iron chair. "I don't think you've ever mentioned what you do for a living?"

CHAPTER NINE

SHE WAS SITTING curled up on the seat across from him, straw hat pulled down over her eyes to shade them from the glare of the overhead lights, one arm wrapped around a matching straw bag. The train was crowded with tourists heading back to *Alexandra's Dream* and the other cruise ships docked at the port. He watched her sleep. She didn't snore, but her mouth was slightly open, her hand propped under her chin, her elbow on the narrow window ledge.

It had been a good evening. They hadn't done anything spectacular, unless having dinner at a street café in a busy Italian neighborhood where seminarians and nuns mingled with shopkeepers and Vatican gardeners almost in the shadow of St. Peter's dome was spectacular, and he tended to think it was. At least when that dinner was shared with a woman like Lola Sandler.

She hadn't complained when it had begun to rain

again in the middle of their meal. Instead, she'd laughed and moved her chair closer to his and insisted they stay outdoors, as steam rose from the pavement and raindrops danced all around them. She'd been as excited as a child when the waiter brought the dessert tray and didn't fuss about the carbs or the calories when he suggested they order one of each of the selections.

She did insist on paying for her own food, and he hadn't argued. And, if going Dutch made her feel more comfortable, then the smirk on the waiter's face that caused a nick to his masculine pride was a small price to pay.

The train slowed as it pulled into the station. Lola stirred and began to wake up. The tip of her tongue came out to wet her lips. She sat up, pushing the hat brim away from her eyes. "Oh, dear," she said. "I fell asleep, didn't I?"

"Only for a little while," he said.

"I hope I didn't snore."

"You didn't."

"Good." She smiled as though at some private joke. "It was all that pasta we had at dinner. It just made me so sleepy I couldn't keep my eyes open."

"I'm glad it was the pasta and not the company," he said as the train shuddered to a halt and people began to stand up and gather their possessions from the seats and overhead racks.

"It was the pasta," she said, moving into the narrow aisle ahead of him. "Definitely the pasta. And the long day," she added as they shuffled their way to the door. "What time is it, anyway?"

He glanced at his watch. "Eleven. We've got plenty of time to get back to the ship." He wondered if he could ask her to join him for a nightcap. She did look tired, but a nice, happy kind of tired. He put his hand on the small of her back as they walked through the station and along the shore back to the pier. *Alexandra's Dream* loomed above, blocking out the sky, the silver and gold moon-and-star logo floodlighted on her smokestack, music and laughter floating down to them. But where they stood in the shadow of her hull, it was quiet and gave an illusion of privacy.

He moved his hand from her waist to her wrist and gave a gentle tug. She stopped walking and turned to face him, her expression slightly bemused. "I wanted to tell you how much I enjoyed our evening before we go back on board," he said. "Once I cross the gangplank I'm on the clock again."

"Oh." A slight frown drew her tawny eyebrows together for a moment. "I forgot you're—"

"Contractually obligated to entertain the paying customers?" he asked, unable to keep a slight edge from sharpening his words.

"Well, yes." Even in the shadow he could see her cheeks darken with a blush of color. "Although, you make it sound like you're some kind of gigolo. You aren't, are you?" He stiffened momentarily before he caught the faint teasing lilt in her voice.

"Hell, no," he said emphatically. "But to tell the truth, sometimes it feels that way when I'm listening to some old, blue-haired biddy ramble on and on about her charities and her ski chalet in Aspen or Geneva or wherever the devil it might be, and realizing I can't just get up out of my seat and walk away from her."

"Does that happen often?" she asked, tilting her head a little so that she could see his face beneath the visor of his hat.

"More often than I like."

"But you must be used to some of it. I mean, the glad-handing and the sweet-talking, rich old ladies. You were on the pro tour for what? Eight years? You surely had to do a lot of that kind of stuff to keep your sponsors happy."

For the first time in hours a tiny warning signal went off in his brain. She worked for a newspaper, he remembered. She had told him that as they ran between raindrops and thunderclaps toward the Borgo restaurant. Reporters were not on his A list. There had been too many of them hounding him after he left the tour, too many unauthorized stories, some of which cut too close to the bone where his relationship with his old man was concerned.

But she wasn't a reporter, he reminded himself. She had said she was an editor for a small newspaper, not *Sports Illustrated*. And for the Women's Page, not the sports section. She had nothing to do with newsgathering. Or with sports. Her ex-husband was a women's college basketball coach. His obsession with his work had been part of why their marriage failed.

He could tell it was a painful admission for her. And he understood her reluctance to talk about her failed marriage, even though he could have told her that her ex's obsession with his coaching wasn't that unusual. He'd seen it happen often enough in his line of work. Coaching a college basketball team couldn't be that much different than playing on the pro tours, or any kind of professional sport, for that matter. It took all your energy, all your concentration, all your heart.

Some people could take the pressure, have a home and family life, and some couldn't. Like his dad. And him. He hadn't wanted to go there, to think about that day at Augusta and the reasons for it, so he'd said what anyone might, that he was sorry about her failed marriage, and nothing more. She said it was a long time ago, over with, forgotten, which he didn't believe, and they'd changed the subject.

Now, looking back on the evening, he realized they'd talked mostly about him, even if it was only surface-level stuff. That surprised him, too. Not that other women hadn't used that particular ploy on him, but that he'd let her get away with it. But when he'd drawn the line past which he didn't want to go, she hadn't pressed. She'd changed the subject and they'd gone on from there. She didn't pout or tease or cajole. There was something different about Lola Sandler. Something he wanted to explore. In other words, he was interested in her brain. And God help him, he was more than a little interested in her body.

He wondered what it would be like to kiss her. And since they were slightly screened from the other passengers making their way along the pier by a huge cement stanchion, he took her in his arms. If she didn't want him to kiss her she'd say so. He'd figured out that much about her. She didn't play coy and she didn't play games. He waited a moment. She didn't move closer, but neither did she back away.

"I'd like to make this night last longer," he said, hitting the kill button on his internal warning buzzer, "but I can't. I was wondering, though. Would you like to join me tomorrow? On Corsica. I'm taking a group for a nine-hole outing in the morning, but the afternoon's my own. There's someplace I'd like to show you."

She raised her arms and set her hands on his shoulders, leaning back a little, letting him take her weight as she looked up at him. The top of her head came just about to his chin, perfect. Not too short, not too tall. And not too round, not too thin—he could tell as he shaped his hands to her waist. She had curves in all the right places, but he could feel firm muscle beneath the skin, as well.

"Not Napoleon's birthplace, right? I mean, that's probably interesting—at least, Frances will think so—but it's not quite what I'd call special." She pulled her lower lip between her teeth a moment then broke out in a smile. "Oh, dear, you're not a Napoleon freak, are you? I didn't spoil it, already, did I?'

He pressed his forehead against hers. "No, I'm not a Napoleon freak. It's a golf course," he said.

She sighed and he felt her nod slightly. "Why doesn't that surprise me? And I know which one. Sperone. It's a Robert Trent Jones Sr. course. They say it's spectacular. Right on the ocean. Like Pebble Beach. My mother read about it in one of my sister's guidebooks. It was one of the few things she's been disappointed about. It's in the south of Corsica, too far for a day trip, isn't it? We sail early tomorrow afternoon, don't we?"

"Yes." He leaned toward her, bringing their lower bodies almost close enough to touch. He could feel the heat of her through his clothes and smell the scent of her skin, flowers and spice and rain. His stomach tightened, sending urgent signals to his lower body. "It's not Sperano. It's called Le Maquis, not so well known, but I'd like you to see it. A friend of mine who used to be on the European pro tour owns it. Rene Picard." He'd had two glasses of wine over the course of three or four hours. That or a beer or two was all he allowed himself, anymore. He wasn't drunk, hadn't been for more than four years, but holding her this way made him feel like he was—a little out of focus, a little fuzzy around the edges—good and ready to howl at the moon.

"I really am a poor golfer," she said, swaying slightly from side to side, her skirt brushing against his thighs, heightening his awareness of how soft and sleek she would feel naked in his arms.

"You don't have to play golf. Just come with me. It's mostly business but there will be some time for us, too." He wasn't sure why he was asking her to accompany him. He'd staked a lot on this chance for a commission to redesign Rene's course at Ajaccio. He should be completely focused on that presentation and nothing else. But he wasn't. It was important, sure, but so was spending time with Lola. And it was growing more important by the moment. The cruise was half over. When it ended she would go back to Ohio.

He had promised Andrew he'd stay on board for two more cruises, three weeks, and by then he hoped Rene would have made his decision on the redesign plan. And, if he didn't give the commission to Eric, then he had some hard decisions of his own to make. He'd been drifting the last year or so and, although his finances were in good shape, he wasn't Tiger Woods by a long shot.

He needed to start bringing in some money. And more than that, he needed structure and goals in his life. He hadn't changed that part of his personality when he'd walked away from golf. He was goal-oriented, always had been, always would be. No matter what he did next, he wouldn't have time to make a trip to the States for several months. By then she would have forgotten all about him. Might even have found someone else. "It will be our last chance to spend time alone together until we overnight in Naples. Will you join me?"

She seemed to think it over. "You're sure I won't be in the way?"

"No," he said, and meant it. "As a matter of fact, you can sit in on the presentation if you want. It'll be very informal. Just me and Rene, perhaps his brother." He'd surprised himself with that one. He hadn't intended to go so far. She could have found something to occupy herself for an hour while he made his pitch to Rene, but now he found himself thinking he would like to have her there beside him. She wasn't an ornament, a diversion, as so many women in his past had been. She was intelligent and perceptive and he'd welcome her input and her critique when his presentation was over.

They had talked a great deal over the past few hours, mostly of trivial things, favorite foods, favorite music. He'd told her about growing up in a country where apartheid was dying a well-deserved death, about surfing in the hunting grounds of the Great White shark, of learning to play golf from his father, who was good but never reached his potential on the tour, nothing more personal than that. But then, with tiny cups of steaming espresso in front of them, cocooned by the falling raindrops beneath their canvas umbrella, he'd told her about his plan to become a golf-course architect and she had seemed intrigued.

Initially, she'd found it surprising, she confessed, that his first step along that career path had been to study landscape architecture, but on second thought, it made sense. She had confessed in her turn that she sometimes had doubts about the course of her life, what she wanted to do in the future, the changes she wanted to make but so far hadn't found the courage to tackle.

"What are the odds your friend will give you the

commission tomorrow?" she asked, returning his thoughts to the here and now and the woman in his arms.

"Better than fifty-fifty, I think. Rene's cautious, but a good businessman and, once he makes up his mind, he follows through. If he does choose my redesign, it will be a real boost for me. I've worked on the designs for two of Cape Town's newest courses, but it's time to strike out on my own. This is my first solo project. Like I said before, the tourist industry in South Africa is booming. And a lot of those tourists want to play golf. There's lots of upgrading and new construction, but it's a true good-ole-boy network, as you say in the States."

"And, like a lot of other careers, it's who you know as much as how much you know, right? You need an 'in.'"

"Exactly. Rene Picard is a Frenchman, and a Corsican, another old friend from my touring days. He retired three years ago and took over the course from his father and uncle. Now he wants to upgrade and expand, maybe attract the notice of the European-tour officials."

"What does one wear to a pitch like this?" she asked, not quite saying yes, not quite touching him with her lower body, not quite bringing her mouth close enough for him to kiss her.

"Proper golfing attire," he said, mimicking a snooty British upper-class accent.

"Good," she said, and her lips were within a heartbeat of his own. "Because I didn't pack a business suit on this cruise. The only thing I have that comes close is too green, the skirt's too short and the jacket's too tight."

"Sounds perfect to me." The thought of her in something too short and too tight did strange things to his insides. "I'm having trouble picturing you in a business suit," he said truthfully. She had looked marvelous and sexy in the slinky black pantsuit the other night. She looked happy and fun-loving in the denim skirt and coral blouse she was wearing tonight—and she would look heavenly in nothing at all. But an uptight business suit and sensible pumps—no way. Her wavy blond hair captured in clips or a bun, her fabulous eyes hidden behind glasses, a clipboard in hand. Never.

"Me, too," she murmured as he gave in to temptation and brushed his lips across hers. "I haven't owned one since I graduated from college and got the job at the *Sentinel*."

Once more the warning bell clamored in his brain but he ignored it. The reality was he could scarcely hear it over the din of the blood pounding through his veins and beating in his ears. So she worked for a newspaper. So what? She hadn't asked to interview him. She was an editor, not a reporter. And he thought he already knew her well enough to trust she'd be up front with him. Tonight, this moment, they were just a man and woman whose minds and bodies were in sync in the here and now, nothing more.

"I'm going to kiss you," he murmured against her lips.

He could feel her smile. "That's what I've been wanting you to do for the last, oh, five or six hours," she whispered, and opened her mouth to his.

CHAPTER TEN

"YOU DON'T HAVE TO BANG around in the dark." Bonnie's voice came out of the deep shadows cast by Lola's berth. "I'm awake. Turn on the light."

"Sorry," Lola whispered, rubbing her knee, which she'd bumped against the edge of the built-in dressing table in their cabin. "Is Fran asleep?"

"She's not asleep. She's not even in her bed. She and Mom are still out dancing."

"Señor Mendoza tonight?"

"They're the hit of the evening, dancing the tango in La Belle Epoque," Bonnie informed her. "What would you think of a Spanish stepfather?"

"I'm trying not to." She was glad her mother was having a good time but she didn't want to think about Señor Mendoza or Father Connelly or any other man except Eric Lashman. Lola sighed as she switched on the bathroom light.

"Don't worry. Fran's with them, playing chaperone."

"Yeah, but what happens after Fran comes back down here with us?"

"Mom and Señor Mendoza will probably go to her cabin for a nightcap." Bonnie's tone implied it might be for more than a nightcap.

"Is he allowed to do that? Go to a woman's cabin like that?"

"Good Lord, Lola. Don't tell me you're going to sic the propriety police on them."

Lola sighed. "I suppose not." Her mother and Señor Mendoza. Her thoughts shied away from picturing them as a couple. She wasn't ready for that. She stepped into the compact bathroom and looked at herself in the mirror. She'd made the right choice in not letting her sister see her face. She looked as if she'd been kissed, well and often. Her lips were slightly swollen and her eyes were heavy with passion. No wonder the purser's assistant, who had passed them through the ship's metal detector when they came on board, had had to fight to keep from smiling. They must have looked like lovers or soon-to-be lovers. Color rose into her cheeks and she touched her fingers to her tender lips.

Was that such a bad idea, becoming lovers? She turned the thought over in her mind. Intimacy didn't come easily for her, but Eric Lashman stirred something deep inside her that had lain dormant for far too long. The part of her that was purely feminine, the part that wanted to be held and kissed and made love to.

She stripped off her clothes and climbed into the shower, standing under the warm spray. She was going to spend tomorrow with him, all day tomorrow. Well, most of the day. She still wasn't going to golf with him.

She wasn't that besotted. Not yet. She washed her hair and dried herself quickly, wrapping her wet hair in a towel. Bonnie might have fallen back asleep and she didn't want to waken her eagle-eyed sister again by turning on the hair dryer.

She opened the bathroom door and stepped into the main area of the cabin. Bonnie wasn't asleep, nor was she pretending to be. She was sitting up in bed, the wall sconces blazing, wide-awake. "So how did it go? Your date with the golf pro?"

"It wasn't a date," Lola said automatically. At least, it hadn't started out that way. It had ended up that way, though. "It was just dinner with an acquaintance."

"Oh, yeah, just dinner. Sure," Bonnie said, her voice dripping with sarcasm. She lay back against her pillows and pulled the sheet up to her chin. "Women don't look like you do when it was just dinner with an acquaintance."

"What, have I sprouted wings? Do I have a tattoo on my forehead?"

"I can smell the pheromones. I'm getting turned on just sitting this close to you."

Lola laughed, half amused, half embarrassed. "What are you talking about?"

"Like they always used to say in Grandma Hilver's romance novels, or was that Clark Gable in *Gone With the Wind*—" She fluttered her fingers over the top of the sheet and simpered, "My dear, you look like you've been kissed." She giggled. "And I do mean kissed. Teeth, tongue and all. Kissed with a capital K-I-S-S-E-D."

Lola opened her mouth but nothing came out. Her sister's words had left her speechless. "How, in heaven's name, can you tell that?" She clamped her fingers around the belt of the fluffy white robe provided by the cruise line so that she didn't give herself completely away by bringing them to her lips.

"You don't get pregnant five times without knowing something about kissing," Bonnie said, laughing once more, and Lola was so happy to see her sister in good spirits that she confessed.

"Okay. You're right. He did kiss me. Until my toes curled and the moon and stars swung in the heavens and angel choirs sang hallelujahs." She flopped back on Frances's pillow. "He is the best kisser I've ever encountered."

"That doesn't surprise me," Bonnie said. "He has the lips for it. Not too thin, not too thick." She rolled over on her side. "Just right?"

"So very right," Lola murmured, her eyes closed, her body remembering the taste and scent and feel of him.

"Oh, boy. You're looking gone, already." Her sister frowned a little and her smile died away. "Just remember it's a shipboard romance, Lola Roly-Pola. Don't get your heart broken."

"I know it's a shipboard romance. Technically, it's not even a romance yet. I've only known the man for what? Seventy-two hours or so? But would it be so very wrong if I did let that happen?" she asked a little wistfully. She was tired of always being alone, of never having anyone to go to bed with, wake up with. To love again. *Exactly as her mother had said.*

Bonnie turned serious. "It would be if you still intend to interview him for the paper."

"Fran told you about my plan to write about him, huh?"

"Of course she did, but we didn't tell Mom."

Lola nodded her thanks. "I don't know, Bonnie. I got an e-mail from my boss. He told me to go for it. I could write a great human-interest piece about Eric, I know I could. He's an interesting guy. He's been all over the world. He practically raised his younger brother by himself. He's taking over his job so his brother can be with his fiancée and their new baby. He wants to design golf courses for a living and I bet he'll be good at it. He walked away from fame and fortune, and never looked back. People want to know what makes a man like that tick."

"He told you all that about himself today?"

"Yes." But nothing about why he had to raise his brother by himself when their father was alive and capable of doing the job himself. Or why he had walked off the course that day at Augusta and away from a lucrative career on the pro tour that reasonably would have lasted another fifteen or twenty years. He'd talked freely about himself until a certain point, and then there had been no more information, only trivia. Lola the woman wanted to know those unshared, personal details of his life, but she held back because Lola the reporter still hadn't made up her mind what she was going to do about the story.

"And you let him share his life story with you, without telling him the truth about yourself?"

"I told him the truth," Lola said, stung. "I told him I'm editing the Women's Page at the *Sentinel*."

"You just conveniently left out the part about that being a temporary assignment, that you're really a sports writer. I guess you forgot that insignificant detail, right?"

"Yes," she said, all the joy she'd been feeling draining out of her heart and dissipating like morning mist when the sun hit it. "I didn't tell him that part. I don't know what I'm going to do, Bonnie."

Bonnie stared at her, eyes darkened with worry. "I

think you'd better make up your mind real soon, Lola, or you might get your heart broken."

"It was only a couple of kisses," she whispered, but she knew her sister was right. Her feelings for Eric were growing by the hour. She was walking a very dangerous path. He was an honorable man. He wouldn't forgive or forget a betrayal like that for a long time. Maybe never.

She didn't want to think about conflicts of interest, anymore. She wanted to climb up into her cozy berth and curl up under the covers and dream of Eric's kisses and what tomorrow might bring. But there was something else on her mind, something that had been there, tucked away in a quiet corner all evening.

She stood and unwrapped the towel. She needed to dry her hair before she went to sleep or it would be standing up all over her head in the morning. "Is that all you did this evening, watch Mom and Señor Mendoza dance?"

"Dinner was excellent. We tried the French restaurant tonight. Fran and Mom had the escargot but I didn't want to tempt the Morning Sickness Demon out of the cave he's crawled into the last day or so, so I passed. Then we went to the show. It was a fifties and sixties review. Mom got a big kick out of it. We met Señor Mendoza on the way out of the theater." Bonnie sounded slightly defensive. "That's when we all went to the champagne bar and they started dancing. I was getting really tired by then so I came back here."

"You said you were going to call Tad when we separated at the restaurant."

"I did?" Bonnie's voice hardened a little. "Slip of the tongue. I meant, I was going to call the kids. I did, a little while ago. They were just getting home from school. We had a good visit. Tad's mom's spoiling them rotten but that's what grandmas are for."

"Did you talk to Tad?" Lola began towel-drying her hair, giving her sister a moment to answer.

"For a little while. We…we didn't have much to say to each other and it costs a fortune for overseas calls," Bonnie finished lamely.

Lola sat down on Fran's bunk again, laying aside the damp towel. "Bonnie, are you still…still thinking about not having the baby?"

Her sister let out a gusty sigh. There was a tinge of sadness in her voice when she spoke again. "I don't know, Lola. I'm so confused. Tad's so upset he still won't talk to me. I mean, I thought I had it all worked out. I'm barely pregnant. It…it will only take a doctor's visit. No one will ever know but me and Tad…and you."

"And Fran," Lola admitted. "I—I told her."

Bonnie reached out and covered Lola's hand with her own. "I know you told her, that's all right. I didn't expect you not to. I thought that I was making the right decision for all of us. Another child to raise. Another college education to pay for. I'm so tired now some days I can hardly stay awake past dinnertime. But now…now I'm not so sure." She started to cry. "What should I do?"

"I can't make your decision for you," Lola said, although she wanted to, wanted to beg her sister to have the baby and love and care for it the way she did her other children. She'd offer to move to Florida and help babysit, give her and Tad all the money she had saved up, but she knew that would only make Bonnie feel worse. Hard as it was, Lola knew she needed to keep silent for the time being. "Please, just promise me not to fuss and worry and talk yourself into a hard-and-fast decision until we get back home. Until you and Tad can be face-to-face and talk this over calmly and rationally. Please, promise me."

Bonnie turned her face to the wall. "I…I don't know, Lola. I…just don't know. I'm so confused."

Lola smoothed her hand over her sister's hair. "Sleep now. It's been a long day. You're tired. No one makes good choices when they're tired. Just sleep, and tomorrow you'll feel better. If you want, I'll stay with you all day."

Bonnie sniffed. "I don't need a nursemaid. I'm not an invalid. I'll be fine. You've got plans and so do I. Fran's signed us up for this private van tour of the island. Señor Mendoza's going with us. He speaks French and Italian, as well as English and Spanish. Did you know that?"

Lola shook her head. Her hair was nearly dry so she decided not to use the hair dryer. Bonnie was looking more and more sleepy. "He deals with a lot of people in his family's sherry business. I did tell you that's what he does when he's not being a host on cruise ships?"

"You mentioned it before." Lola still didn't know if she believed that one. Why would a successful sherry exporter spend his spare time dancing with widows and rich divorcées? What kind of a hobby was that? A hobby that let you cruise the Mediterranean, eat gourmet food at every meal and meet interesting people, she admitted to herself with characteristic honesty.

"We're going to the house where Napoleon was born, and whatever other moldy old buildings our guide hauls us to, and then we're driving out into the countryside to a farm where they distill medicinal plants into essential oils. Corsica is covered with a particularly aromatic plant, 'maquis', they call it, although it just looks like scrub land to me in the pictures."

"That's the name of Eric's friend's golf course. Le Maquis. Now I know what it means."

"It was also the name of the French resistance fighters in the Second World War," Bonnie supplied, then burst into laughter when they both said, "according to Fran" at the same time.

"Supposedly, they have an age-old tradition of making medications from indigenous plants on the island," Bonnie continued when she'd stopped laughing. "*Aromatherapie* is how you say it in French. I'll buy you some and we'll try it out."

"Thanks," Lola said, still smiling.

"After that we're going to a vineyard to have an authentic Corsican meal and wine tasting. I'll eat too much, because they say the food's very good, and maybe I'll even have half a glass of wine," she finished defiantly, then yawned hugely.

"Promise?" Lola asked softly.

"Cross my heart," Bonnie said, and Lola could hear a smile in her sleepy voice once more. "And so you don't spoil your day worrying, I'll make sure Mom and Señor Mendoza behave themselves, too."

CHAPTER ELEVEN

LOLA WANDERED AROUND the small landscaped patio that adjoined the clubhouse of Rene Picard's golf course, then settled at a round iron table beneath a gaily striped canvas umbrella. She hadn't spent so much time sitting out of doors beneath umbrellas since her honeymoon in Cancun. Which she tried never to think about anymore. It was nice to have new memories of bright sun and blue skies and umbrellas to overlay the tarnished ones of four years ago.

She picked up her camera and snapped a couple of shots of the purple-and-white flowers growing in a container set against the wall, glad she'd given in to her older sister's insistence she borrow the small digital for her day trip while Bonnie shared Myra's camera. She was getting some good shots that her mother and sisters would enjoy seeing. She was especially pleased with the photos she'd taken of Rene's family homestead, hidden from view behind a ridge that encircled the small valley where the course was laid out.

She had spotted the farmhouse from the van window on the way in and followed a path up the ridge to get a better look after Eric, his young Czech helper, Milo, and the dozen middle-aged and elderly golfers in their charge teed off. The house itself was large, the roof steeply pitched with six dormer windows. The fieldstone lower story, enclosed by a low stone wall, had turquoise shutters and flowers growing in profusion over it. There was a barn, equally large, and a number of smaller out-buildings. Sheep grazed over the hillside and horses ran in a paddock by the barn. She would have loved to explore farther, hiking up into the hills, but she wasn't dressed for serious hiking and was unfamiliar with the trails so she sensibly stayed put on the clubhouse patio, whiling away the time drinking cold tea and trying out a few words of French and Italian on Lily, the shy young waitress Rene Picard had assigned to look after her.

The patio was empty, and there were no other patrons on the course or in the dining room. The silence was broken only by unfamiliar bird calls and the sound of the van's idling motor in the parking lot as Eric and Milo loaded the golfing party for the ride back to the ship. She and Eric would be returning later, courtesy of Rene's nephew, in plenty of time for the ship to sail.

The sun was high and beat down on the cobbled patio with single-minded intensity, but a sea breeze had found its way inland and cooled her underneath her umbrella. She let her thoughts wander wherever they wanted while her eyes focused on the ancient gnarled olive trees that bordered the fairway and lifted silver-gray branches toward the sky.

In some ways, the clubhouse and grounds reminded her of the municipal courses and small private clubs back home. The clubhouse was long and low and consisted of a pro shop and kitchen and locker rooms backing a bar and restaurant that looked out onto the first tee. But that's where the similarities ended. This wasn't flat, green Ohio farm land, with grain silos off in the distance and strip malls lining the roadway. The building was native stone, echoing the farmhouse and its outbuildings. The eighteen-hole course was carved out of an ancient olive grove, bordered on one side by the maquis and the other by the foothills of Corsica's mountainous interior. She counted half a dozen mountain peaks, each one higher than the last as they marched off into the distance. And that view was so spectacular and so changeable as clouds passed over the sun that she took three more shots of it, even though she had at least a dozen, already.

After viewing the new shots and deciding they were too spectacular to delete, Lola put aside the camera and inhaled deeply, breathing in the heady aromas of eucalyptus and wild thyme, rosemary and sage, and the unfamiliar scents of the flower beds edging the waist-high wall that bordered the patio. A few dozen feet away a fountain bubbled merrily in front of the flowering hedges that screened the service sheds and greenkeeping equipment, grouped out of sight at the edge of the parking lot.

It wasn't a grand fountain like the ones she'd seen in Rome. It was rustic and moss-covered with benches around its basin and water pouring out of a jumble of stones as though from a rocky mountain spring. But the sound was soothing and the sight of the falling water added to the illusion of coolness provided by the lattice-covered patio. Golf carts, lined up off a graveled path near the pro shop door, awaited the arrival of a group of VIPs, some midlevel French minister and his entourage visiting from Marseille. Rene had apologized for the unexpected company when he'd greeted Eric's party.

The minister's last-minute visit had only been announced the day before, giving Rene no opportunity to inform Eric their time together would have to be curtailed. She could tell Eric was disappointed but she doubted any of the other passengers enjoying their morning of golf had noticed anything was wrong.

Rene Picard came through the glass sliders of the dining room and walked toward her. He was a compact man in his midforties, only an inch or two taller than she was, with broad shoulders and powerful thighs. His skin was the color of milk chocolate and his hair was cropped so closely to his skull it looked like it had been painted on his head with a brush. He wore khaki slacks and a dark blue shirt with a pale blue tie that her intensive shopping on the Via Condotti told her had been made by Armani. He looked casually elegant and completely at home in his surroundings. "Is there anything I can get for you while we're waiting for Eric?" he asked in heavily accented English.

"No, thank you. I'm still full from lunch. It was excellent. My compliments to the chef." There had been grilled fish with a sesame butter sauce and lamb shanks flavored with rosemary, along with grilled vegetables and artisan bread from Rene's family's farm. Dessert had been sticky honey cakes and fresh fruit, and she was afraid she'd made a pig of herself when she couldn't resist a second helping of both.

Lola motioned for Rene to sit down and he took the seat beside her. "I could get used to this," she said with a smile. "This view, these smells. It's heavenly." And she meant it.

Rene accepted her compliments with a wave of his hand and a smile that showed strong white teeth. "Corsica is called the Scented Island, you know. It's said that Napoleon always boasted he could tell the island of his birth even blindfolded by the smell of the maquis."

She took another deep breath. "I understand what he meant. Is this building part of the original homestead? It appears to be very old."

Rene nodded. It was originally stables. My great-great-grandfather was an avid breeder."

"It's very nice but not as spectacular as the house and barn on the other side of the ridge."

"My family home. It is over two-hundred years old."

"Who lives there now?"

"I do. Along with my brother and his wife and my nephew and his family. I am divorced and my children are away at university. One in Paris the other in London." He saw the look of surprise on Lola's face. "It is a very big house, you see."

"You are lucky to have such a lovely home. I envy you. Am I right in thinking there are some great hiking trails in those hills?"

"Yes, and some good fishing higher up. And off the coast. There are a great many things to do in Corsica."

"I'm learning that. I wish I had more time to spend here."

"Then, you must return, soon, and be my guest at Le Marquis," her host said graciously.

"Thank you, I hope I might return, as well."

Rene had been carrying a long plastic tube when he

came out of the dining room. He laid it on the table between them and held up his hand for a moment, listening. "Ah, it sounds as if the bus for the ship has left. Good. Eric should be joining us momentarily."

"You've looked over his plans for the redesign?" she asked, hoping she wasn't overstepping any boundaries by asking.

"Yes," he said, grinning. "I like what I have seen so far. I'm just sorry Eric and I won't have more time to discuss the plan. Once the bus leaves the grounds, no one else will be allowed in here until our honored guest has played his round. He is due to arrive by helicopter in thirty minutes." His words were sharp-edged as though his true opinion of the government official was less than favorable.

"Will Eric and I be allowed to leave?" she asked. She wasn't a worrier…usually, but she didn't want to miss the ship. It was a long way to Naples, their next stop.

"I have made arrangements for my nephew to drive you out, but I had to talk a good game to get you permission to stay until the minister arrives." As he spoke, as if on cue, half a dozen very large men rounded the hedge from the parking lot. They weren't in any kind of uniform but they might as well have been. They couldn't have been any more conspicuous and out of place than they were in their dark suits and white shirts. They wore earpieces attached to cords that disappeared down the backs of their necks and their suit jackets bulged in odd places. They looked exactly like a French version of the U.S. Secret Service and, of course, that's exactly what they were.

"Agent LeSatz and his men. They are D.G.S.E., our version of your Secret Service. There have been threats lately from the usual groups against French officials. Better to be overly cautious than not cautious enough."

The serious-faced agents spread out around the area, although none of them came close to where Lola and Rene were sitting. Rene ignored them, turning his attention to the plans before him. He spread them out on the table and smoothed them with his hand. "I like what Eric has proposed. He isn't trying to turn my little venture into a second Sperano." He laughed. "There's no way that will happen."

"I've never seen Sperano," Lola admitted, "except in pictures. I know it's a spectacular course, but the views here are lovely, also."

Rene bowed his head in a gracious nod. "Thank you. I think so. My family has owned this land for two-hundred years. I'd like to dream that, one day, Le Maquis might be a stop on the European tour, but that will take time and more capital than I have to invest at the moment. Corsica isn't as developed a tourist destination as the rest of France or Italy. But I think, and my family agrees, that we can make a success of a small development here. An inn, tennis courts, a swimming pool." He waved his hand in an all-encompassing gesture.

"But to make a success you need a course that will appeal to the average golfer as well as the professional." Lola looked up to see Eric, accompanied by one of the silent bodyguards, approach their table.

"I see you've started the presentation without me," he said with a smile, although Lola was beginning to know him well enough to discern a slight tenseness in his shoulders and at the corners of his eyes. This was the way he would be before a tournament, she realized:

Confident but not arrogant, slightly aloof, laser-focused on playing well and winning.

Rene rose to his feet. The two men clasped hands and then Rene leaned forward to give him a very Gallic hug and kiss on the cheek. "I was telling Mademoiselle Sandler my dreams for Le Maquis. I was just getting ready to show her your design, but now that you're here you can do the honors."

The bodyguard interrupted Rene with no appearance of regret. He spoke rapidly in French and Lola didn't understand a single word, but his body language was easy enough to read. He wanted them off the patio and he wanted Lola and Eric off the premises.

Rene's answer was just as short and to the point.

He turned to Lola and Eric and raised his shoulders in a shrug. "We have fifteen minutes," he said. "They wish to make a last security sweep of the area. Politicians," he added, making it sound like a dirty word.

"Those guys look like they mean business," Eric remarked as Agent LeSatz moved off a few feet to confer with his colleagues, who had now produced what appeared to be metal detectors of some sort and were sweeping the bushes and flower beds along the edge of the patio.

"There has been more unrest than usual this summer," Rene said. "We have separatists here on the island," he explained to Lola. "Corsica has not always been part of France. There are some who want it that way again."

"Don't these groups usually go for foreign-owned targets?" Eric asked as he leaned over the table, anchoring the edge of the drawings with his hand as a gust of herb-scented breeze ruffled the pages.

"Usually," Rene agreed, and his face darkened momentarily. "But like many situations, the rules are changing. New elements are coming into the mix. It's no longer just our own home-grown separatists with a marker in the game. Organized crime is involved. Sometimes it turns violent. Sometimes innocent Corsicans get caught in the middle." He looked over his shoulder at the six men going about the grim business of sweeping the outbuildings for explosives. Lola gave an involuntary shiver. "Sometimes we do what we don't want to do to stay on the right side of the politicians." This time Lola didn't have to imagine the scorn in his words. It was more than plain to hear.

"I see." She didn't, of course. She had enough trouble understanding American politics, and there was very little or nothing of Corsican affairs in the news broadcasts.

Rene seemed to understand. "But the violence is not intense. And seldom in this part of the country. Enough of politics," he insisted. "We're wasting our time." He stabbed his finger at the drawing Eric had placed on top of the pile. "You think we can redesign the first three holes and move the clubhouse to the farm?" he said, narrowing his eyes as he studied the detailed drawing. It wasn't a computer rendering, Lola realized, but hand-drawn and beautifully done. Eric was a talented artist, a skill she hadn't known he possessed until that moment.

Lola leaned forward and saw where Eric had drawn in the farmhouse and its outbuildings, adding a loggia-covered patio and umbrella tables much like the ones where they were sitting at the moment. She drew in a breath, taking in the changes the reconfiguration would bring to the course. The views of the mountains, impressive now, would be enhanced by the sweep of orchard and meadowland that surrounded the centuries-old farmstead. "The house has eight bedrooms, enough for a very exclusive inn."

"But that would leave my family homeless," Rene said facetiously.

"The upper storey can house you all quite comfortably with some judicious remodeling."

Rene nodded. "My brother and I have discussed this possibility. Continue."

"Even with the upgrades needed for the kitchen and dining room, it will be less expensive than building from the ground up. And the ambience is unbeatable. Couldn't be reproduced in new construction no matter how much money you spend. Add a swimming pool, hot tub and tennis court, integrated into the back of the house, and you have yourself a very exclusive golf getaway."

He was right, Lola realized, picturing the farmhouse she'd seen in the distance as a welcoming weekend getaway. She could see Rene was imagining the same scene she was. As she listened, Eric and Rene continued discussing the pros and cons of lengthening the sixth hole to take advantage of a stream meandering through the property, and the option of designing a "dry" water hazard instead of trying to alter the stream's course to produce a small lake, far more practical for such an arid climate.

She watched as Eric swept his strong tanned fingers over the drawing, countering Rene's argument that the course needed to be lengthened to attract the ever-increasing range of the professional players' long game.

"Rene, I know your long-term goal is turning Le Marquis into a tournament venue, but don't lose sight of your day-to-day profit model. A successful, income-generating business, a full-service destination for overnight guests, amenities for day-trippers. That's not necessarily incompatible with a tournament venue, but ninety-five percent of the golfers that come here will not routinely hit three-hundred-yard drives. Far from it. What they need is a natural, intelligent, challenging course, not monster holes. You've got the bones of that right here. My redesign plays to your strengths, and to the future."

From the corner of her eye Lola saw the security detail leader approach once more. At the same time she heard the distinct, stomach-vibrating thumping of helicopter rotor blades. Rene and Eric seemed oblivious to both distractions, but the security agent wasn't to be denied.

"You must leave now," LeSatz said, this time in English. "Or you will remain in the clubhouse under guard until Monsieur Dupré has finished his game."

"Merde," Rene muttered loudly enough for the man to hear, although he pretended not to. "I'm sorry, my friend. But I would like to keep these drawings, study them, discuss them with my family, if I may. You have given me much to think about even in this short amount of time. You're right, my mind is too attuned to the tour courses. My dream may be to see Tiger Woods play at Le Marquis, but my bottom line says I should be thinking of the golfing enthusiasts like those you brought with you today from *Alexandra's Dream,* who will pay the bills and keep this beautiful place in my family's hands for the next two-hundred years." He began to carefully roll Eric's designs and replace them in the protective tube.

"What I've tried to give you here is the best course possible for the site," Eric said with simple conviction. "All I ask is that you keep that in mind as you consider your decision on whether or not to go with my design." They shook hands again and once more Rene wrapped his arms around Eric's shoulders in a hug.

"I will do just that, *mon ami,*" he said. "Exactly that."

The helicopter drew closer. The kitchen door opened and Lola saw Rene's chef and the dining room staff, including Lily, arrayed in its frame, watching the helicopter approach. One of the security men was making a last sweep of the fountain as Rene took Lola's hand and lifted it to his lips. Shocked, she had to stop herself from jerking her hand away in surprise. He gave her a quick light kiss on the back of her hand and said, "You are always welcome at Le Marquis and in my home. Please return to us soon."

"Thank you," Lola said, touched by the invitation, but uncomfortable with the courtly gesture. It might look romantic on TV and in the movies, but in reality it was embarrassing, at least for her. "I have enjoyed myself very much today."

"We must leave now," the agent insisted, his tone curt. Eric took Lola's arm and prepared to follow the bodyguard off the patio. They had moved only a few yards when the helicopter swooped over the ridge that hid the farm buildings and dropped down onto the grass at the edge of the parking lot. The rotor blades beat the air like horizontal windmills and stirred the dust of the graveled parking lot into a maelstrom of dirt and stones.

Lola half turned away to protect her face and eyes from the stinging grit and then everything seemed to happen at once. The security man who had been sweeping the fountain began to yell, gesturing to his comrades to move back from where they were standing. Lola couldn't hear what he was saying over the roar of the helicopter's rotors, and couldn't understand the French words, anyway, but she could see the look of fear on his face.

Agent LeSatz's hand sliced the air, ordering the kitchen staff back into the building. Rene moved toward his employees at the same time, yelling in Corsican and French, brandishing the heavy plastic tube with Eric's drawings inside like a sword above his head.

"What's going on?" she tried to ask as she felt Eric's arms come around her, pushing her to the ground behind the shelter of two huge stone flower pots.

"There's a bomb in the fountain," Eric shouted, dropping down beside her, covering her body with his own as the entire patio seemed to erupt into heat and flame and noise.

CHAPTER TWELVE

STONES AND WOOD and mortar rained down onto the loggia, shredding the leaves of the hibiscus that twined over it like colorful thatch, splintering the latticework roof. The glass sliders to the dining room shattered into millions of tiny pieces as shards of stone blasted across the patio. Lola's ears rang like gongs but she could still hear screams of pain and fear above the roar, and she struggled to be free of the heavy weight that made breathing the stinking, dust-laden air harder than ever.

"Let me up," she said, pushing at Eric's shoulder. He didn't budge, didn't move a muscle. For two more agonizing breaths she wondered if he might have been badly injured or even killed. Her heart began to hammer even louder in her chest and she struggled to be free. "Eric? Are you okay?" she shouted, but it came out barely louder than a croak. She felt him shift his weight and lift his head to look over the massive stone urns that had absorbed most of the energy of the blast, and the deadly rain of stone that had once been Rene's fountain.

"Stay put," he commanded.

She didn't have much choice; his lower body was still pinning hers to the flagstones. "What happened? Was it a bomb?" It seemed incredible to her, unbelievable, but what else could it have been? A meteor falling from the sky? A lightning strike? Not likely. There wasn't a storm cloud within a hundred miles. Eric ignored her questions. He rested his hand heavily on the top of her head, keeping her from looking around. Someone, a young girl, from the sound of her voice, started screaming hysterically. It was Lily, Lola realized with horror; the shy little waitress had been standing in the open doorway when the bomb had gone off. "Eric, let me up. People are hurt."

He shifted his hand from her head to her shoulder. "Are you okay?" His dark hair was full of stone dust and there was blood on his cheek from a cut at the corner of his eye.

"I'm fine," she said, her stomach jumping from fear and the sight of the blood running down his cheek. She started to cough, choking on the smoke and dust that swirled around them. "Are you?"

"What?" He lifted his hand to his face. It was bloody, too, from a cut on the back of his wrist.

She grabbed his arm. "Your hand."

He looked down, wiggled his fingers. "I'm okay. It's not broken." He pulled a handkerchief from the pocket of his slacks and wrapped it around his wrist. "Can you stand?"

"I'm fine," she said. He wiped at the blood on his cheek with the back of his hand. She reached out to stop him. "Wait. I have some antiseptic wipes in my bag."

She looked around but didn't see the woven tote she'd left on the back of her chair. Then she spied it lying under the twisted remains of the table she'd been sitting at moments before, a very large piece of stone pinning it to the patio flags. She swallowed hard against another wave of nausea. If she hadn't moved from that spot she'd be dead, or at least very badly injured.

"Later," Eric said curtly. "It's just a scratch, like they say in the movies."

"What happened?" she asked, still breathless, pulling Bonnie's camera out from under her hip, where she'd landed on it. She was going to have a bruise. A big one, but that was the only damage she could find. Eric's body had protected her from any further harm.

"I don't know for sure. A bomb, I think. Not a big one, thank God, or we'd all be dead."

This time when she got to her knees, Eric didn't try to stop her. She peered over the edge of the big stone urn, afraid of what she would see. "Oh, God," she breathed. The security man who had been sweeping the fountain lay facedown against the stone wall. Two of his companions were kneeling beside him, guns drawn. Agent LeSatz, his suit covered with dust, but otherwise seemingly unharmed, sprinted toward them. Another agent was running toward the helicopter, gun drawn.

The helicopter hovered six feet off the ground, its rotors creating a whirlwind of debris. Lola hid her face against Eric's shoulder and wished she could stay hidden behind the flowerpot until it was all over, but she couldn't ignore the moans and cries for help coming from the kitchen.

"Rene!" The anguish in Eric's voice communicated

itself to Lola, arcing through her body like acid along her nerve endings.

"Where?" she asked, struggling to her feet. Her hip was stiff and painful but she limped along behind him without complaint. His friend was lying beneath an overturned table and broken umbrella, Eric's tube of drawings a foot or two from his outstretched hand. "Oh, God," she whispered, "let him be all right."

Eric moved quickly, dropping to one knee beside the prostrate man. Lola jerked on the straps of her tote, pulling it free of the stone. Rene was going to need much more than antiseptic wipes, but she had a scarf in there, too. It would do for a tourniquet if they needed one, she thought, dredging up bits and pieces of information from a long-ago Red Cross course she'd taken.

She hurried up behind Eric, glancing past Rene to the whimpering and bloody young couple in the door of the kitchen. It was, indeed, Lily who had been injured, her face and throat bloodied by shrapnel. Lola picked her way through the debris toward them, realizing as she did that, although Lily's cuts and scrapes were bleeding profusely, no one appeared to be seriously hurt.

"Are you okay?" she asked when she reached them. Lily broke into a rush of speech that sounded more Italian than French. It must be Corsican, Lola surmised. She'd never heard it spoken before that day. The girl broke down sobbing again. Her companion—the bartender, Lola recalled as she tried to place his bruised-and-battered face—turned to her and replied in blessed English.

"She is okay. The chef has gone to fetch water and bandages. But Monsieur Picard? I—I think he is badly hurt."

"My friend will look after him." She pulled the

packet of wipes from her tote and handed them to Lily's companion. "These might help."

"*Merci, mademoiselle.*" She gave the boy—Armand, was his name, she remembered suddenly—a pat on the shoulder and rose to her feet. The helicopter had climbed to a few hundred feet and disappeared toward the north. The air had started to clear. Smoke was rising here and there from burning tufts of dried grass, but otherwise there appeared to be no fire. Water still spouted from the ruined fountain, raining down on the far corner of the patio, moving downhill toward the motionless security agent and spreading out across the flagstones.

The sound of the helicopter intensified and she could see that it was returning. LeSatz noticed, also. He rose from his crouch, talking into a small microphone attached to his lapel. The agent who had been knocked to the ground was sitting up now, and Lola breathed another sigh of relief. He was pale and held his left arm at an awkward angle, but he was conscious, at least. The side of his face was scraped raw and reddened by burns.

She turned her attention to Rene, who had begun to stir. "How is he?" she asked Eric, raising her voice above the helicopter's noise.

"I am okay," the injured man groaned. "Get this table off me." Eric picked up the edge of the heavy iron table with one hand and shoved it away as though it weighed no more than a feather. Rene rolled over and covered his eyes with his arm. He moaned and reached his free hand toward his knee. "Damn, my leg. I think it's broken."

"I'm sure it's broken," Eric growled. "Lie still and I'll see how bad it is." There was blood on Rene's pant leg and Lola flashed back to the stomach-wrenching pictures of compound fractures she'd been forced to study in that long-ago college course.

Eric reached into his pants' pocket and came up with a penknife. He slit Rene's pant leg from thigh to ankle and pulled it apart. Lola let out a sigh of relief. The blood was from a really nasty cut on Rene's knee and not from a wound caused by shattered bone protruding through broken skin.

"You'll live to golf another day," Eric said, relief evident in his voice. "Do you think you can sit up?"

"I don't know," Rene said. "Is the sun circling that olive tree or is it just my poor head?"

"It's your head," Eric said. "Better lie still."

"My chef? My staff?"

"Cuts and bruises for the most part," Lola informed him. "I'm going back to check on them again in a minute."

"Only Armand, the bartender, speaks English."

"Good," she said. "All the French I know is 'How much is that?'"

Rene managed a strangled laugh that ended in a groan.

"I'll make sure someone's calling 9-1-1," she said. "Or whatever they call it in Corsica."

She hurried back to the kitchen door and noticed, for the first time, that it was steel and had shielded most of the gawking staff from the blast. Armand had helped the still hysterical Lily to her feet and set her down in a chair that someone had pushed over from one of the tables. She was holding a cold compress to her head and not crying quite as hard as before. Behind her, the chef, massive and dark-skinned, his white hat askew, his coat splattered with blood, held a cell phone to his ear. He made a gesture Lola didn't recognize but one that said as plainly as words that he had the situation in the kitchen under control.

"We're doing okay," Armand clarified. "The emergency patrol is on its way. Along with the police and fire brigade. How is Monsieur Rene?"

"He has a broken leg, a nasty cut above his knee and a big knot on his head. Otherwise, I think he's okay."

"It was the separatists," Armand continued, accepting a new compress from the sous chef for the injured girl. "Damned government... How do you say? Flukies?"

"Flunkies?" Lola ventured.

"Flunkies." She could see him store the word away for future reference. "Why do they need to come here, anyway? Why can't he play in France or at Sperona where all the big shots go? We don't want trouble here. Now see what has happened?"

"Mother of God," the sous chef sputtered, pointing behind him. Both Lola and the bartender spun on their heels. Eric was still kneeling, supporting Rene against his shoulder. Two uniformed French soldiers had jumped out of the helicopter followed by a tall, thin man in golfing clothes who leaned out the open hatch but didn't exit. Behind him Lola could see two very pretty young women in shorts and halter tops, and then another man, pudgy and bald. The soldiers were carrying automatic rifles at the ready. The security men rose to their feet, supporting their comrade on a sling made of their crossed arms, as the soldiers began moving toward them.

Suddenly, the small bald man shouldered the two women and the blond man aside and began waving his hands, gesturing wildly, his face red and his mouth wide-open as he yelled orders. To the soldiers or the pilots, Lola couldn't tell which, but the soldiers stopped walking, hesitated for a moment, then began backing toward the copter.

The engines revved once more. It was going to take off and leave the wounded agent and the others behind. Anger rose like bile in her throat. She couldn't believe what she was seeing. Perhaps there was some kind of rule governing the agents, but there were innocent civilians who needed to be evacuated to medical help. The helicopter slowly began to rise as the soldiers hopped up into the hatch.

Instinctively, Lola lifted her camera and pushed the on button. She began to snap some shots. She used the view finder instead of the LCD screen because her hands were still shaking too hard to hold it steady enough to see what she was shooting. It took her a moment to remember which way the zoom worked, and, when she put the camera to her eye again, the wounded agent was being waved off by the bald man.

"Bastard," the sous chef shouted in French, shaking his fist. Even Lola had no trouble with that translation.

"Flunkie!" Armand yelled.

"Asshole," Lola muttered under her breath.

Once reminded, Lola continued to take pictures. She was a sports reporter, after all. Action shots were second nature to her. Point and shoot, no time for framing or artistic composition. She snapped a shot of Eric helping his friend to his feet, and then another of him amid the broken glass and overturned furniture, speaking to LeSatz as they placed his wounded agent on a chaise with a cushion less damaged than the others.

She took a couple of pictures of Rene's kitchen staff huddled around Lily. The chef, arms crossed, stood guard over his flock amid a pile of shredded canvas umbrellas and hibiscus blossoms that had been torn from the overhead vines. The waitress was crying again so Lola turned off the camera and went to see if there was anything she could do to help. But there was little more assistance she could offer. She was an outsider who didn't speak the language and she had no medical training. Lola felt more than useless as she hovered at the edge of the action.

Eric called her name and she turned to him in relief. "Get some clean cloths for this cut, will you? And see if one of the waiters will help me splint his leg."

"Here, take this," Armand said, thrusting a stack of clean white linen napkins into her hand. "Napoleon, here, will go with you. He is the strongest among us."

Napoleon? Lola thought. Well, why not? The Little General had been born on this island, hadn't he?

"Thanks," she said breathlessly as a tall, bronzed young man with shoulders as broad as a linebacker's rose from a crouch beside Lily, whose sobs, thankfully, had dwindled away to hiccups.

For the next ten minutes Lola was kept busy holding the pad of a pressure bandage to Rene's bleeding knee and keeping the metal slats of a ruined umbrella in proper alignment to splint his broken leg. Eric used her brightly colored scarf to stabilize the splint, giving Rene's leg a rather jaunty look.

When she looked up from her task, she saw that they had been joined by two men who bore a striking resemblance to Rene—his brother Philippe, and his nephew, she learned. They had been working at the farm with half a dozen others, the course's greenkeepers, who had been sent away for the day to comply with the rules laid

down by the security agents. They were followed shortly
by the village constable and fire brigade. The firemen
and the constable began a survey of the damage and
made sure there was no chance of a fire from leaking
gas or downed electrical wires. Not a moment too soon
someone found the valve that supplied water to the
ruined fountain and turned it off. The patio was nearly
awash and Lola's shoes were soaking wet.

"At least the rest of my employees were not in harm's
way," Rene said.

Now that the shock had worn off, Lola could see he
was in a great deal of pain, as was the injured security
agent who had been burned by the blast and whose
shoulder and right arm had been broken when he was
blown against the stone wall.

"How long before the ambulance gets here?" Eric
asked as Rene's brother finished a conversation on his
cell phone and flipped it shut.

"Ten minutes, perhaps a little longer. The village
nearest us does not have an ambulance. It's coming
from Ajaccio and it is a thirty-minute drive."

"I could use some brandy," Rene groaned, leaning
back against the pile of chair cushions his nephew and
Armand had fashioned for him.

"He could have been in hospital by now," Rene's
nephew said with quiet anger, "if our esteemed guest
had not flown off like a coward."

And left his own injured man behind, Lola thought,
but didn't say out loud.

"The French should stay in France. But why would
the brotherhood target us? We are good Corsicans."

"Enough." Rene silenced his nephew with a gesture
of his hand. "We don't know who was responsible for

this damnable bomb. The brotherhood is not what it once was. Nothing in the world is as it once was."

Lola and Eric exchanged glances. The little she knew of Corsican politics was that some people had separatist leanings, and there was an occasional bombing or, more rarely, a shooting.

"Lola, go sit down," Eric ordered. "You look like a ghost."

She did feel shaky all of a sudden. A siren could be heard off in the distance and she realized with relief that the ambulance was finally coming. She righted a chair and sank into it. Armand offered her a glass of wine but Erik waved him off and asked for water, instead. He stayed beside her while she drank it and, almost immediately, she felt better, less likely to float off into the sky and fall asleep on a cloud. "Thanks," she said, "I needed that."

"You've been great through this whole mess. A lot of women—" He stopped abruptly.

"A lot of women would have gone all girlie on you," she said. "Like that poor little waitress?"

"Sorry. I know that's not politically correct, but that's been my experience in the past with most women."

"Well, I'm not most women, but just between you and me, I wouldn't have minded sitting down and bawling my eyes out," she admitted with a tired smile. "I still could."

"Lola." He reached out a hand and smoothed her hair behind her ear. He never finished what he meant to say because at that moment the ambulance arrived and a squad of E.M.T.s, under the command of a formidable gray-haired woman who looked to be about Myra's age, swarmed out of the vehicle and began fanning out across the patio. Even Agent LeSatz couldn't talk his way out of being checked over by the diligent rescue workers. Eric had his wrist and cheek bandaged. Lola was made to look up and down and count fingers to make sure she didn't have a concussion. Lily, who had cried herself into exhaustion, was also bandaged and sent by car with Napoleon to the village clinic.

Rene's splint was pronounced sufficient for the ambulance ride to Ajaccio, and he and the injured bodyguard were loaded into the vehicle. "Eric," Rene called from his nest of pillows. "I want my nephew to take you to the docks. There is nothing more you can do here and, if you don't leave soon, you will miss your ship."

"No way, buddy. Not until I know there's nothing more wrong with you than a busted leg and a lump the size of an ostrich egg on that hard Corsican skull of yours." Eric grasped his friend's hand and covered it with both his own.

"Your concern for Monsieur Picard is admirable," Agent LeSatz said. "But I'm afraid you won't be able to accompany him to the hospital. I haven't completed my investigation of the bombing. You are not free to leave Le Maquis until I say so."

The village constable stood behind the French agent, nodding his head in agreement.

"Our ship is leaving in less than an hour," Eric said, his jaw tightening. "As an employee of Liberty Line, it's my duty to see that Ms. Sandler is returned to the ship in good time to sail with her family."

"I'm sorry. This is a terrorist incident involving a member of the French government. My authority takes precedence over sailing schedules. However, I will do the best I can to see that you are reunited with the ship in her next port of call if you do not arrive in time to sail with her."

"The ship spends tomorrow at sea," Eric said. She could tell he was angry beneath the icy calm he seemed to be able to call forth at any time. His "game face," she was coming to think of it. "Her next port is Naples, Italy," he added for emphasis.

Lola had risen to protest LeSatz's order. Now she sat down with a thump. "Oh, no," she said, and really thought this time she would break into tears. "Italy," she said, horrified. "My passport." She looked up at Eric, blinking hard to hold back exhausted tears. "I forgot it on the ship."

CHAPTER THIRTEEN

"CAPTAIN PAPPAS, I can't believe what I'm hearing. Why is it not possible to hold the ship for forty minutes until my daughter and Mr. Lashman can make it to the quay? Surely, a ship this powerful can make up that small delay and still make Naples on time tomorrow." Myra Sandler's voice shook with the intensity of her feelings. Mike O'Connor had to admire the woman's pluck, even though he wished she were wailing and hysterical and turning to him for guidance and support during this crisis. His calm, steady counsel would get him back in her good graces faster than all the sweet talk he could spout for the rest of the cruise.

Instead, he was standing awkwardly behind her, knowing full well he was trespassing on Nick Pappas's private domain. The ship's bridge was off-limits to everyone but essential personnel. He'd never figured to get himself up here, but Myra Sandler wasn't taking no for an answer, even from the master of *Alexandra's Dream*.

"Of course we could make up the delay easily," the captain said smoothly. "That's not my point." He paused a moment to add emphasis to his next words. "I'm sorry, Mrs. Sandler. I believe I have already explained this to you. There has been a terror alert issued for the port as a result of the bombing at Le Maquis. It is my duty to remove my ship and her passengers and crew from harm's way as expediently as possible. There is no alternative."

Myra's backbone lost some of its starch. Her shoulders sagged. "None at all?" she asked.

"It is my duty," Pappas said with finality.

Mike had to admit it. In his spotless white uniform and four gold stripes on his sleeve, Nick Pappas looked every inch the veteran sea captain. His bearing was professional, his skill handling the big liner unmatched. But there were a few skeletons in his closet just like everyone else's, and Mike had made it his business to find out what they were.

"Captain, we are ready to sail," Giorgio Tzekas whispered in the captain's ear, a patently false smile of sympathy on his face as he gave the Sandler women a nod of greeting.

Tzekas and Pappas were both in their late thirties, Greek, with dark hair and eyes, but there the similarity ended. Pappas had earned his stripes through hard work and experience. Tzekas's father, on the other hand, had bought his two and a half stripes for his wastrel son. And now it was Mike stuck with keeping the screw-up out of trouble, and both of them out of hot water with the Boss.

"But Father Connelly told us that most of the bombings on Corsica are carried out by groups who only want to protest against the government," Myra insisted, regaining her fortitude. "They don't target tourists. My daughter and Mr. Lashman were merely in the wrong place at the wrong time. I'm sure the ship's in no danger. Isn't that right, Father?"

Mike winced. He wished Myra hadn't brought his name up, calling the captain's attention to his presence. Nikolas Pappas was not one of his biggest fans. Mike had caught the man watching him with speculative interest more than once on the uncomfortable occasions when he was required to dine at the captain's table or their paths crossed on deck, a circumstance he did everything in his power to avoid. The master of *Alexandra's Dream* was not a man to cross even at the best of times, which this definitely wasn't.

Half an hour earlier Myra had met him at the door of her cabin in a state of great excitement, her two older daughters looking equally worried and upset behind her. "What's wrong?" he'd asked immediately. It was odd enough that she had had him paged. She hadn't exactly been avoiding him since Rome, but she was decidedly less friendly than she'd been before. It was odder still that she'd asked him to come to her cabin. Not that he wouldn't have enjoyed an invitation under different circumstances, but he figured Mendoza had cut him out of the hunt, and since he had his triptych to console him, he wasn't as disappointed with the widow and her possible "donation" slipping through his fingers as he might have been on another cruise.

"Lola hasn't returned to the ship," she had said, the stones in her rings flashing in the afternoon sunlight as she'd ushered him inside her spacious cabin, which would have made three of the broom closet he occupied.

"There's been a bombing at the golf course where she went with Eric Lashman."

"My God," he had said, making the sign of the cross. "Are they okay?"

"Yes. I just finished speaking to her. She called on some French Secret-Service Agent's cell phone. I didn't know the French even had a Secret Service, did you?"

"Momma," Bonnie'd said, "that's not important."

Myra'd fluttered her hands again. "I know. I know. I'm rambling. But I'm upset. My daughter could have been seriously injured or killed. It's such a shock. A terrorist attack. I remember 9/11. Those awful pictures on the TV." Tears had sprang to her eyes and Frances'd come forward to put her arms around her mother's shaking shoulders.

He wished he had thought of it first.

"They're both okay, Father," Frances had explained as Myra'd attempted to pull herself together, "although there were others who were injured. The problem now is that Lola and Mr. Lashman have been delayed. They're being interrogated by the French and the Corsican authorities. They won't reach the port until after we sail."

"I'm afraid I have no authority—"

"We need to talk to the captain, Father," Myra had interrupted. "I want him to hold the ship for them."

He should have just told her then and there to save her breath. That wasn't going to happen. No way would Nick Pappas hold the ship to wait for two passengers. And Mike was right. They'd been standing on the bridge of *Alexandra's Dream* for the last fifteen minutes arguing. Any other time he'd be thrilled to be up here; the place fascinated him. It was as high-tech as a NASA launch site and even more off-limits to the likes of him.

"Please, Captain. I'm begging you." Myra hadn't raised her voice but Mike could tell she was close to losing the last of her composure. He stopped gawking at the bridge and started paying attention to the wealthy Florida widow once more.

Nick Pappas must have sensed her breaking point was at hand, too. His voice softened. "Mrs. Sandler, I am responsible for the health and safety of more than fifteen-hundred souls. I cannot hold the ship. I am sorry, but that is my last word. I must ask you to leave the bridge at once. We must cast off. Tzekas," he said, without turning his head. "Make ready. We sail on my order."

"Yes, Captain." Tzekas signaled to a crewman, who began to punch a series of commands into a computer display. Mike spared a glance for the ship's huge teak wheel, which somehow didn't look as out of place as it should amid all the electronics and LED displays.

"My sister doesn't have her passport." Bonnie spoke for the first time. "How will she be able to leave Corsica without a passport?"

"Corsica is a region of France," Tzekas explained as Pappas turned away with a murmured apology to sign off on some kind of log presented on a clipboard by a female officer. "The American consul in Marseilles can issue her a new passport."

"Marseilles? She has to go to Marseilles?"

"I'm afraid so, Myra," Mike said, patting her shoulder. "It's the closest consulate."

"How will she get there? How long will it take to issue a passport? I waited weeks for mine and I was in the States."

"Once she gets to Marseilles, by plane or by ferry, she can have her new passport in a couple of hours' time," Tzekas said. "Then she and Mr. Lashman can fly to Naples and meet the ship there."

"Captain Pappas?" Myra's voice broke but Mike saw her take a deep breath and, when she spoke again, she had herself back under control. "Is this really the only way for my daughter to return to the ship?"

"There is a possible solution that just occurred to me. If you can secure your daughter's passport and take it to the Purser, we can send it back to the port authority with the pilot boat and she can retrieve it there. That will at least save your daughter the trouble and expense of a trip to Marseilles. I regret that is the most I can do." Myra opened her mouth to protest but Nick Pappas held up his hand. "And that will have to be done quickly. The pilot will leave the ship in twenty minutes precisely. Now, ladies, if you will excuse me, I have a ship to sail."

"I HAVE NEVER BEEN so thankful to see anything in all my life," Lola said, taking the dark blue passport with its embossed silver eagle from the unsmiling harbor pilot. "Thank you so much. *Merci. Merci.*"

"My pleasure, *mademoiselle,*" the man said, his voice more friendly than his expression.

She turned to Eric, her face luminous. "I can't tell you how I dreaded flying to Marseilles. I'm so glad we don't have to make the trip." She smiled, but even that couldn't hide the exhaustion that darkened the hollows beneath her eyes and tugged at the corners of her generous mouth. "I've never been stranded in a foreign country before. It's nerve-racking."

"Almost getting blown off the golf course is nerve-racking, too." He tried not to smile. She was prickly where her dignity was concerned.

"I agree with you there. But from now on I take this with me everywhere." She slipped her passport into the zippered pocket of her tote. "Where's yours?"

"Both of them are in here," he said, patting his pocket.

"Both of them?"

"I have dual citizenship," he explained. "My brother and I were born in the States. One thing I learned while traveling on the international tours was to never let them out of my possession. You never know when your luggage is going to turn up missing, or get stolen or you miss your flight. It's a habit after all these years."

"It's a habit I'm going to cultivate from this day on. Now what do we do?" She looked around the spare, dun-colored, cinder-block room in the harbormaster's office, where they'd been waiting for the pilot boat.

"The ferries out of here go to Nice and Marseilles," he said, thinking out loud.

"That's the wrong direction," Lola observed, a little frown drawing her brows together. "I've spent the last two hours trying to avoid going to France."

He nodded. "There's another option. We can try for seats on a late flight out this evening. I made some calls while you were confirming your ID with the harbormaster."

"Where's that flight headed—Timbuktu?" she asked sharply, her exhaustion fraying the edges of her voice.

He forced himself not to smile. "Not quite that far.

To Naples. I went ahead and booked the seats, but it will make a late night for us. We could try for a couple of rooms here, if you'd rather." He hoped not. He hadn't just gotten them seats on a flight to Naples, but secured them a place to stay, as well.

"I'd rather not spend the night," she said, looking down at her clothes, a swingy wraparound skirt and cotton top. Her skirt was muddy from kneeling on the flooded patio. There was a dark stain at the hem that was Rene's blood, and her blouse had a tear in the sleeve. "I look—" She threw up her hands at a loss for words. "Like I've been through an explosion. And I smell like it, too. Will they even let us on the plane? We look like—" Words failed her.

"Getting on the plane won't be a problem," he said, considering their appearance for the first time. His clothes were in worse shape than hers. "It's a private plane. A friend of Rene's and mine is making it available to us. His pilot is flying in from Nice. We have another hour until we have to be at the airport. This is a tourist town. Let's shop."

She stood up, giving him one of her glorious smiles. "Now you sound like my sister and, for once, I'm not going to argue. But I do have one more question. Is it possible to find someplace to clean up? It isn't only my clothes that are filthy. So is the rest of me."

They'd spent hours at the hospital waiting for word of Rene's condition and being debriefed by Agent LeSatz. Eric didn't want to spend any more time smelling and looking this way, and he was a guy. It would be ten times worse for a woman.

"We can shower on the plane."

"Private plane. Big enough for a bath with a shower.

We're not talking someone's four-passenger Cessna, are we?" She tilted her head slightly and narrowed her eyes.

"Not quite," he said, letting the smile show this time. "It's a Gulfstream 5. And there's a small apartment on the coast that comes with it."

"The coast. The Amalfi Coast?" She wasn't beautiful, not by a long shot, but when she smiled the way she did at that moment, it took his breath away.

He nodded. "It's in Positano. Is that okay with you?"

"Okay? It's fabulous. The Amalfi Coast. Positano. *Under the Tuscan Sun* Positano?"

"And a whole day to enjoy it. The ship doesn't dock until Wednesday morning. Tomorrow they're at sea, remember?"

She laughed. "Maybe this isn't going down in history as the worst day of my life, after all."

CHAPTER FOURTEEN

SHE HADN'T REALIZED how wonderful it felt to be clean and dry and to have her hair smell of flowers and spice and not dust and smoke. She was so tired she could barely keep her eyes open but she couldn't sleep. Might not be able to sleep at all for the rest of the night. She was in Positano on a balcony on a hill high above the town. She had never dreamed of staying in a place like this. The air smelled of flowers and the sea, and church bells rang out the hour all around her.

The sky was ablaze with stars, the sea a blanket of black velvet spread out toward the horizon and dotted with fishing boats with lights attached to their bows to lure anchovy and shrimp to their nets. Eric was pouring wine from a bottle he had found in the small wine safe in the apartment. She could hear him moving around behind her. She leaned her elbows on the intricately designed wrought-iron railing and considered for the first time what rarified circles Eric had once moved in. Obviously still could if he wanted to.

Rene's friend, and Eric's, as well, was another professional golfer. His name would send her mother's blood pressure soaring to dangerous levels when Lola told her she had not only flown in his private jet, but spent two nights in his pied-à-terre in one of the most beautiful spots on earth. Lola had never met anyone wealthy enough to own their own jet. Or their own golf course, until today. And Eric could be one of them. He had been good enough. He had the talent to have risen to the top of his profession, but one day he had turned his back on it all and walked into anonymity.

Why? The reporter in her wanted to know.

And even more urgently, the woman in her wanted to know.

"Here's your wine," Eric said, coming through the French doors to the balcony. "Would you like something to eat with it? I found cheese and olives in the fridge and a box of some kind of hard little bread squares, or crackers, in the cupboard."

"No, thanks," she said as he handed her the glass. She took a sip. The wine was cool and crisp and she sighed in contentment. "I hope this helps me sleep. I'm so tired I can barely keep my eyes open, but my mind is still going a mile a minute. And the drive down here from Naples didn't help. I know it's breathtaking in the daylight, but at night it was absolutely terrifying."

"I know what you mean," he said, taking a swallow of his own wine. "And I was doing the driving." He was teasing her and they both knew it. He was an excellent driver, handling the narrow road and the hairpin turns with ease, even when the thought of the sheer drop into the sea and the motorcycles passing on either side of the car had Lola clinging to the door handle.

She took another sip of wine, watching him over the rim of the glass. He was wearing a pale blue shirt, the sleeves rolled to just below his elbows, and dark slacks that made his waist and hips look even slimmer than usual. His hair was still damp from his shower and lay in waves across his forehead. He stood with one hand on the balcony railing and looked out over the village to the dark sea. A breeze cooled the night air, chasing away the heat of the day. From someplace nearby she could hear music playing on a radio, soft and romantic and exotically Italian to her American ears.

She wrapped her arms beneath her breasts and swayed to the music. She had chosen a flowered sundress in shades of lime and teal and a lightweight, short-sleeved sweater in soft white wool to replace her ruined clothes on their whirlwind shopping spree in Ajaccio, and for the next day, a pair of shorts and a silky T-top. She had felt too dirty and disheveled to try the dress on in the shop, but the saleswoman had chosen the size well and she felt pretty and feminine enveloped in its silky folds.

Eric took another swallow of his wine as he looked down over the edge of the balcony at the quiet street below them. At least, she guessed you would call it a street. It was so narrow and steep that there was no way anything bigger than a minibike could navigate it. They'd left the rental car they'd picked up at the Naples airport in a private garage on the cliff above them— garage space was measured by the square inch in this cliffside town, according to Eric—and walked to the apartment. She was glad she'd bought rubber-soled sandals to wear with the dress instead of the strappy heels the saleswoman had pressed on her. This was definitely not the town for high heels. There were stairs everywhere. From what she'd seen so far, nothing except for the beach was flat.

"It's getting late," Eric said after a few more moments of silence between them. "You should try to get some rest." He wrapped his hand around the stem of the glass, drawing Lola's attention to the bandage on his wrist. The doctor at the emergency room in the small hospital in Ajaccio had wanted to put stitches in the cut at the corner of his eye but Eric had refused, allowing the frowning young doctor to apply only a butterfly bandage.

"I will in a little while. Were you able to contact Rene's nephew? I saw you talking on your cell phone a few minutes ago."

"I did speak with him. Rene's resting comfortably. His nephew said the only way they could get him to stay the night was to promise he could go home first thing tomorrow morning. It doesn't look like he's got a concussion. That's what the doctor was worried about. The leg's a clean break. That cut on his knee will probably give him more trouble than anything. They have to work the cast around it."

"I'm glad it's not more serious. Did he have any new information on the employees at Le Maquis?"

"Everyone's okay. Don't know about the Frenchman, of course, but those military types aren't very forthcoming."

"Did anyone claim responsibility for the bomb? I mean, don't those kinds of groups usually do that?"

"Rene's nephew didn't know who set the bomb.

Maybe he didn't want to. It's a small island. Everyone has to get along. It's a complicated situation."

"We'll probably read about it in the papers tomorrow," Lola said. The tiny but elegant apartment on the third floor of a narrow, centuries-old building didn't have a television or a phone.

He shrugged. "It might make it into the Rome papers. Maybe not. Sadly, this kind of incident happens now and then on Corsica. It just usually doesn't target Corsican property, or be so badly timed that people are endangered like today. Mostly the bombs go off at night. When no one's around."

She shivered, wishing she'd worn the little white sweater out onto the balcony. "I hope in this case the bomb went off prematurely, and that it wasn't an indication of an escalation in violence."

He lifted his glass in a salute. "I'll drink to that. *Salute.*"

"*Salute.*" She finished the wine and looked at the empty glass a little wistfully.

"Another?" he asked. "You've probably earned it."

"No," Lola said, and then with a little more emphasis declined a second time. "Thank you, no. I tend to snore if I drink too much. It's a family trait. And this apartment, absolutely charming as it is, is far too small to torture you with my snoring." She could feel her color rise. She was talking too much. "But don't let that stop you from having another glass. Unless you snore, too?" She tilted her head slightly and looked boldly into his eyes, charcoal now in the heavy shadows of the flower-draped balcony.

He laughed and set down his glass on the balcony railing. Before she quite realized what he was doing, he reached out and pulled her into his arms. "Lola, you are unlike any other woman I've known."

Her heart was thumping so hard in her chest she could scarcely breathe. She had caught herself wondering what it would be like to be held in his arms again. As she had suspected, it was even more unsettling and more enticing than it had been on the quay in Rome. Tonight he was coiled like a spring about to go off. She could feel the tension in his steel-hard muscles. He smelled like the herbal soap she'd found in the bath, a kind of sandalwood, or something equally exotic and alluring, almost erotic. Or perhaps that was just Eric himself, all male, sexy as hell. She willed herself not to let the tremors that raced along her nerve endings communicate themselves to her voice.

"Because I'm honest enough to tell you I snore when I'm drunk?" she asked, hoping to keep things light. She had the feeling that, if he leaned down, put his lips on hers, kissed her, she would lose all her power of reason and drag him into the little apartment and onto the huge bed that took up half the room.

"There's that," he admitted, leaning just a little closer, tipping her head back so their lips were only inches apart. "And because you hung in there through a terrifying day. And because you're here with me when you could have insisted we find a hotel in Naples and stay put until the ship makes port."

"Why stay in a cookie-cutter, noisy hotel in a busy city when we can be here," she said, her voice so constricted she could barely form the words. If he didn't kiss her soon she was going to kiss him first, and what would he think of that?

"Why, indeed?" He did kiss her then, gently at first, then with more firmness, parting her lips with his tongue, coaxing her to open to him. Her arms came up and circled his neck. His hair was soft and silky against her fingers and the kiss held even more magic than their first.

She let his tongue invade her mouth, let his kiss grow deeper and more intimate, closed her eyes and just let herself feel. It had been so long, so very long since she had been kissed this way, as if she were the most desirable woman he'd ever held in his arms, as if he couldn't get enough of her, or she him. The kiss seemed to go on forever, his arms splayed across her back, his head blocking out the stars and the heat of his body warming her to her core.

And then it was over, and she was left feeling suddenly bereft. He leaned his forehead against hers. His breathing was fast and shallow and she was secretly pleased to feel his heart hammering against the palm of her hand. "That was some kiss," he said, his voice as ragged as his breathing.

"I'll say it was," she managed in a whisper. Her lips were tender, her breasts tingled with heat and need that were fast spreading to other more private places. "Is there a limit on how many we can share?"

"Yes," he said, putting an inch or two between their bodies. "Tonight there is. And that was it."

She felt like crying, or screaming in frustration, or just grabbing the front of his shirt and pulling his mouth down on hers once more. "Why so?" she finally managed to ask, not quite able to meet his gaze head-on. Had it been that bad? Had she heard him wrong? She hadn't done a lot of kissing lately but she'd never had any complaints in the past.

"If we keep this up we're going to end up in bed together, and I don't think that's what you want." He shoved his hands into his pockets and took a step back, almost disappearing into the shadows of the bougain-villea that draped the lattice roof of the balcony.

"How do you know what I want?" But deep in her heart she understood he was right. That hadn't been an ordinary kiss. No man she'd ever kissed, including her ex-husband, had set her insides alight that way. It wouldn't take more than another one or two and she'd be ready to throw caution to the wind and climb onto the big soft bed with him.

"I understand you well enough to know you're not a one-night-stand kind of woman."

"But I might be an *Affair To Remember* kind of gal," she said, wanting to reach out and smooth the lock of hair that had fallen over his forehead back into place. Instead, she curled her fingers into her palms and stayed where she was.

"Not tonight," he said quietly. "It's time for bed, Lola. It's been a hell of a day for both of us. Let's get some rest."

She sighed. The single glass of wine she'd drunk had gone straight to her head. She was exhausted and keyed up and not thinking straight. She'd known this man less than a week and she was ready to hop into bed with him. That's wasn't like her at all. "You're right. I'm too tired to think straight. Tomorrow—" She cleared her throat, feeling suspiciously close to tears. "I wouldn't want to do something we might both regret tomorrow."

He nodded, still standing in the shadows with his hands shoved deep into the pockets of his slacks. She almost smiled but stopped herself in time. Her spirits rose slightly. He wasn't as unaffected as he was pretend-ing. If he was trying to hide his erection, it wasn't work-ing. There was no mistaking his arousal. He wanted her—as much as she wanted him.

"I'll grab a blanket and a pillow and sleep out here on the chaise," he said. "You take the bed."

She didn't argue with him. He was an old-fashioned kind of guy. It was a matter of honor with him for her to have the bed. Fine, she wasn't that die-hard a feminist. "Thank you. Sleep well, Eric." She turned to go inside.

Tomorrow. She would wait and see what the morning might bring. After all, they had another whole day to spend together in one of the most beautiful and romantic places on earth. Another day.

And another night.

CHAPTER FIFTEEN

"FATHER CONNELLY, I thoroughly enjoyed your lecture. I'm so looking forward to visiting Pompeii tomorrow. It's practically the entire reason I booked this cruise. I'm just mad to see the body casts of those poor doomed souls, and try to imagine all that hot stone and death just raining out of the sky—" Gloria Broadman gushed. There was no other description for it, Mike O'Connor thought sourly. The words just poured out of her mouth without letup. "Of course, it's so horrible all those people dying like that." She clicked her tongue against her teeth. Capped, he decided. False, just like everything else about her. What possessed a fiftysomething woman to have breast implants, anyway?

"Very tragic," he mumbled, reminding himself she was worth a lot of money, and since he'd wasted the first half of the cruise sweet-talking Myra Sandler to no avail, he couldn't afford to be choosey when another mark presented herself. "But we've learned so much from the excavations of the site, that perhaps they didn't all die in vain." He glanced around the quiet ship's library hoping for rescue from one of the other lecture attendees, but they seemed to have scattered to other venues on *Alexandra's Dream* as soon as the question-and-answer period was finished. It was far too beautiful a day to be indoors.

"Exactly so," Gloria continued, angling her head a few inches to better view the photos of the erotic murals of the lost city's largest brothel, which he'd pulled off the Internet to spice up his lecture. "So, so sad. You will make room for me in the group you lead on our tour, won't you?" she asked with what he imagined she considered a flirty pout.

Mike sighed. "Of course," he said with a smile as false as her cleavage. The henna-haired witch from Cleveland had attached herself to him the moment the ship left port in Rome. Maybe he should rethink this priestly masquerade? The women he was attracted to weren't the kind who had flings with priests. The ones who did…well, they were the Gloria Broadmans of the world. But a fellow had to earn a living somehow. He reached out and took her plump hand in his, looked her straight in the eye and turned on the Irish charm. "Tomorrow I am all yours."

She giggled like a schoolgirl and gave him a quick peck on the cheek. "I'll hold you to that promise. Now I have to go. I have a spa appointment. I want to look my best tomorrow."

"Nothing they can do at the spa can improve on perfection," he lied through his teeth.

"Oh, Patrick, you shouldn't say such things." But

the sparkle in her eye and the arch tone of her voice told him he certainly must if he wanted to see a nice fat check for "his boys." "I'll see you at dinner. You will join my friends and I, of course." Another command delivered as an invitation.

"I would be honored to." She was traveling with three of her former college roommates, all as artificially enhanced and intellectually vacant as she was. Dinner would be a true penance.

He watched her leave the library, threading her way through the rows of folding chairs, ample hips swaying seductively.

Mike watched her go, and sighed. The cleaning crew would be in shortly to stow the folding chairs that filled most of the library's free space. There'd been thirty people in attendance for his "Death of a City" lecture, including Myra Sandler and her two older daughters, relieved enough to enjoy herself once again now that she knew her youngest was safe and would rejoin the ship in Naples. Nice crowd. Good audience.

He enjoyed this part of the gig a lot. Maybe his next persona would be as a history professor at some small backwater college. He would manufacture a curriculum vitae for Professor Michael O'Connor and settle down somewhere to live off the proceeds of the Albanian monks' icon.

Mike felt eyes on the back of his neck and turned to see Ariana Bennett watching him from behind her desk, her vivid blue eyes wary. He gave her his best smile but she only nodded her head and went back to the notes she'd been making throughout his entire lecture. What the hell was she writing about? His well-honed larcenous instincts were on full alert. If he got a chance he would take a look. Maybe it would give him a clue to the whereabouts of the Greek and Roman antiquities her father was supposed to have helped smuggle out of Italy before his death.

Did she have any suspicion he was checking up on her? She didn't like him, didn't trust him, and he was more than half convinced she had taken the missing shard of the shattered Greek vase he had stashed away in a drawer in his broom-closet-sized cabin.

"Ariana Bennett. Ariana Bennett. Report to the Accounting Office, please." A disembodied female voice came over the speaker in the corner that broadcast the ship's messages in properly discreet tones.

"You're being paged," Mike said, moving toward her, his tone affable, his face serene while inwardly he was dancing a jig at this unexpected opportunity.

"I can't imagine why," Ariana said, taking the iPod's tiny headphones from her ear. "I really shouldn't leave the library unattended with the cleaning crew scheduled to come in."

"I'll keep an eye on them," Mike said as casually as he could manage. He hadn't figured on an opportunity like this dropping into his hands anytime soon.

"I—I don't think so."

"We don't want any more accidents," he reminded her, letting anger seep into his voice, then looking immediately contrite.

"I know." She sounded more than a little distracted as she slipped the notebook into the top drawer on the left-hand side.

"But if the cleaning crew doesn't get in now, who knows when they'll be back? These chairs could be cluttering up the room all day. Go ahead. I'll keep an eye on the place. It's probably just some computer glitch with payroll, but you don't want to be held up in port tomorrow, do you?"

"No," she said, seeming to make up her mind, "I don't want to be held up. I'm hoping to spend the day ashore tomorrow."

"Ah, Pompeii. Have you ever been there before?"

She slipped the iPod into her bag and anchored it on her shoulder. "What? Pompeii? Oh, of course. I can't wait to see the ruins."

She wasn't a very good liar. He wondered what she was really planning to do when they docked in Naples tomorrow morning. Something to do with the scribbling, he imagined.

"Go see what the bean counters want," he said, urging her out the door. "Don't worry about the cleaning crew. I'll be right here."

He shut the door behind her but didn't go immediately to her desk. He'd been in the business too long to let impatience lead him into a trap. The last thing he wanted was for Ariana Bennett to get a hundred feet from the door and decide she had to come back and get her precious notebook, and catch him red-handed riffling through her desk drawers.

So, when the library door opened ninety seconds later, he didn't even jump, merely turned from surveying one or two of the better replicas in his little collection to confront whoever had entered the room. "Tzekas," he said, letting the mask of affability drop. "What the hell are you doing here?"

The first officer looked around, nodding with satisfaction to find the library deserted except for the two of them. "Don't worry about me, O'Connor. Why aren't you looking through the bitch's desk? I didn't arrange to have her called down to accounting so you could stand there with your finger—" He lapsed into Greek but Mike had no trouble translating the insult.

"Take it easy," he growled. "I don't want her sashaying back in here and finding us both with our fingers…in the cookie jar." But he moved to the desk as he reached inside the pocket of his cassock for the lock pick he seldom ever left behind if he thought he'd have reason to visit the library. *Be Prepared* was Mike O'Connor's motto as well as the Boy Scouts'. He sat down and gave the surface of the desk a quick once-over. Nothing out of the ordinary—a blotter, pencils in a cup, a stapler, a house phone and desk lamp, just the usual. He slid the end of the lock pick into the lock and began to jiggle it ever so gently. This needed to be a finesse job, no smash-and-grab today. Thirty seconds later, the lock clicked open.

"We're in," Mike said.

Giorgio was at his side in the blink of an eye. "Hurry," he said. "I need to get back to the bridge. That damned Nick Pappas has been on my ass all day." Tzekas was as Greek as feta cheese but his command of American slang was impressive. "What's in there?"

"Not much. Here's the notebook she's been writing in." Mike picked up the spiral-bound book and began to look through the pages.

"What the hell…" his partner muttered. "Is that Greek? I can't read a word."

"It's ancient Greek. She probably figures no one else on board can decipher it. That's why she left it behind. Lucky for us I can read a little." He kept on reading as he talked, doing his best to make sense out of the unfamiliar words and handwriting. He skimmed over the written pages searching for relevant words and phrases. "It's notes mostly. Bits and pieces. She must keep the originals on that iPod she's always got with her. Evidently she's looking for information on the site at Paestum."

"Paestum?" Something in his partner's voice alerted him but Mike didn't stop what he was doing.

"That's the site her father was accused of stealing artifacts from by the Italian government."

"And it's where we get some of our best pieces."

Mike shut the notebook and replaced it exactly where he'd found it. He'd seen enough. He closed the drawer very carefully and heard the locking mechanism click home. He slipped his lock pick back in the pocket of his cassock and stood up. Giorgio had been looking over his shoulder as he read. He began to straighten lazily, only to be jerked upright when Mike grabbed him by the knot of his necktie and pulled his face close, so that they stood toe to toe and nose to nose.

"That's where we get some of our best pieces? Have you taken delivery of a new shipment and forgotten to tell me about it? Are you holding out on me, Tzekas? Your daddy's money won't be able to save you if you're holding out on me."

"I'm not holding out on you. What gave you that idea?" But he couldn't hold Mike's gaze.

Damn, the greedy bastard was going to get them both arrested, or worse yet, killed.

"You'd better not be. We're playing with the big boys this time around and, as far as I'm concerned, there's no honor among thieves. If you're holding back a piece for yourself, it had better show up in my cabin in the next sixty minutes—" He let the threat trail off into silence. The vaguer the threat, he'd learned over the years, the more fear it engendered in weak minds.

He released his grip on the younger man's tie and smoothed the knot back into place. "Now get out of here. If Ms. Bennett comes back and finds us together, it won't take her long to put two and two together."

"The Bennett bitch is going to Paestum tomorrow," Tzekas said, both hands flat on the desk, his eyes full of anger and a glint of fear. "I think we had better alert our contact there that she is on her way. Let him handle her."

"Fine," Mike said. He smoothed his hand down the front of his cassock. He hoped the librarian had enough sense to keep her mouth shut when she got there. He didn't wish her any harm, but there was still the issue of the missing piece of the broken vase. If she had it, then she was a threat to him and she needed to be dealt with.

"If she has an accident at the dig site, it would be tragic, of course," Giorgio said with mock sympathy. "But archeological sites are dangerous places. Especially for a woman alone. Accidents happen, is that not so, my friend?"

"You'd better get out of here before she comes back. She's suspicious of me, already."

"But not of me," the first officer said, all but preening.

God, the jackass would end up getting them both killed. If he got through this with a whole skin, Mike vowed, he'd never work with a partner again. He was too old for this crap.

"She doesn't care enough about you to be suspicious," Mike said. The door opened. Tzekas stiffened but didn't turn around.

"Who is it?" he mouthed.

"Gloria," Mike said, wondering what in hell else could go wrong that day, "did you forget something?"

"Oh," the woman said, attempting another flirty pout, "I'm sorry, I didn't mean to interrupt."

Giorgio gave her a small, courtly bow. "You are not interrupting, madam. I was only checking with Father Connelly to make sure his collection is being cared for to his satisfaction."

"The crew's attention has been first rate," Mike said with his own little bow.

"Excellent. Then I will be about my duties. Father, you will let me know if there is anything more I can do." Giorgio gave Gloria a glistening white smile and marched out of the room, his back ramrod-straight.

"My, what a handsome young man," Gloria said, her eyes lasered in on his butt.

"What can I do for you?" Mike asked, wishing he were anywhere else in the world at the moment.

"Why, I came back to ask the librarian if she had anything on Pompeii my friends and I could read up on this afternoon. We're all so excited about tomorrow. We can't seem to get enough information." She looked around, her eyes wide. "But she's not here?"

"She only stepped out for a few moments. She'll be back shortly."

"But with you here I don't need to wait. Isn't that convenient? I'll bet you can tell me lots more about Pompeii than she can." She looked around and then gave him one of her toothy smiles. "And isn't it marvelous? We seem to have the entire place all to ourselves."

CHAPTER SIXTEEN

"I DIDN'T THINK it was possible to find a more spectacular view than we had at breakfast, but this is truly breathtaking. I thought places like this only existed in movies and romance novels." They were sitting in the shade of a grape arbor terrace belonging to a family-owned trattoria in a tiny village tucked away on the top of a cliff, accessible only by foot. They had driven up from Positano in the relative cool of the early morning as far as they could go, then hiked along the cliffs above the town until they came to this storybook medieval village.

They had visited its small church with its pink stone convent attached by a covered walkway. There were no nuns living there now, according to their guide, an elderly man as rough-edged as the cliffs around him, but the former convent was kept as a hostel for travelers, and the gardens and vineyards, now run by a village cooperative, were open to the public. And their wine was served at both the village's restaurants, and even in Positano and Amalfi, where it was much in demand, he boasted. He even gave them a tasting, so Lola bought two bottles for her mother for Thanksgiving, and lit candles in the church for Rene's and Lily's recovery from their injuries.

After their sightseeing trek, she and Eric had returned to the little trattoria for a lunch of cucumber, goat cheese and olive salad, served with a loaf of crusty hearth-baked bread. Now, as the afternoon heat grew oppressive, they were content to sit under the grapevines, cooled by the sea breeze and to watch the ever-changing colors of the water far below. "I don't want to leave. Ever," Lola said, taking just one more picture of the gray-green cliffs with their crowns of towering white thunderheads, perspective making them appear to be marching off into the distance along the coast. "Even if it doesn't smell as good here as it did in Corsica."

"I think someone down the way is keeping chickens in their backyard," Eric agreed, wrinkling his nose.

"Well, nothing's perfect. It smelled heavenly at Rene's place yesterday and someone tried to blow us up. I can put up with a little whiff of chicken now and then if everything else stays peaceful and quiet."

Eric laughed, a low pleasing rumble that slipped along her nerve endings like little electric charges, setting off echoing fireworks deep inside her. He was sitting with one arm over the back of his chair, sleeves rolled above his elbows, his collar opened to reveal a sprinkle of dark hair. The bandage around his wrist was very white against his tanned skin, and there was some bruising around the cut at the corner of his eye, which, oddly enough, only added to his air of roguish appeal. On the other hand, the bruise on her hip was pure ugly. It didn't look roguish or anything else. A big old bruise, purple and green and thankfully hidden by her shorts.

"You look very pleased with yourself. What are you thinking?"

She wasn't about to tell him that she was thinking all he needed to look like a pirate king was a three-cornered hat and a cutlass. "I was just marveling that twenty-four hours ago we were in fear of our very lives, and now all I can think about is that I want fish for dinner. It's surreal almost, isn't it?"

"I agree." He paused a moment as if he, too, were mulling the change in their circumstances. "I know of an excellent restaurant in a cove just down the beach," he said. "The fish they serve comes straight off the boats that tie up at their dock. Will that satisfy your craving?"

One of them, she thought, but didn't allow herself to speak the words out loud. He'd awakened darker and more passionate appetites within her and they were growing stronger by the hour. "Only if it's my treat," she said, with a bit of a challenge in her voice. "To thank you for getting us through this with class and style."

He ignored the compliment but answered the challenge. "You're expecting an argument from me, aren't you?" he asked, taking a swallow from the bottle of mineral water. She watched his throat work and thought of how the muscles in the strong column of his neck and shoulders had felt under her hands the night before and had to swallow herself before she could reply.

"I thought I might get one."

"Well, you won't. I'm a twenty-first-century man,

perfectly willing to let a woman buy me dinner. If you'll let me buy you a drink, first."

"You're not getting an argument from me, either. I can compromise. I'll be ready for another glass of wine by dinnertime."

"You can have your wine, but I was thinking of limoncella. We can't leave Amalfi without you tasting it. They make their own at the restaurant I mentioned."

"Limoncella? It sounds luscious."

"It's a liqueur made from locally grown lemons. You mentioned *Under the Tuscan Sun*. There was a scene where they drank limoncella in that movie."

"On the beach," she said as the image dropped into her conscious mind. "I remember. But I'm surprised you've seen the movie. It's definitely a chick flick."

"When you spend almost a month in an eight-by-twelve cabin with closed-circuit TV, you watch what they show," he said dryly. "Amalfi is famous for making the liqueur. My soon-to-be sister-in-law says it tastes like a lemon drop dissolved in vodka."

"Is that your opinion, as well?" She tipped her head so that she could watch his expression, but, as usual, he had his emotions under control and all she could see was a slight hardening around his mouth.

"I think you might like it," was all he said. "We can walk to the restaurant if the tide's low enough and you're not too tired, or they have a boat that will pick us up at the marina."

"Let's take the boat. It's more…adventurous." She'd almost said romantic but caught herself in time. "Will you join me in a glass when we get there?" she asked, wondering what his reply would be. He drank very little, she'd observed over the time she'd known him. She was still reporter enough to wonder if he was simply a tee-totaler, or if there was another reason for his abstinence.

His smile disappeared completely. He looked past her at the latticework loggia that shaded the main dining area of the trattoria from the hot August sun. "I found out a few years ago that I can't handle my liquor as well as I thought I could. I think I'll pass."

"But you didn't stop drinking completely?" She indicated their empty wineglasses, which the waiter, who also appeared to be the chief cook and bottle washer, hadn't yet taken away from the table.

He nodded. "I guess it's my way of staring down the beast, of keeping control. My drinking probably wouldn't have affected my game or my health for years, but I knew it would eventually. I could see what was happening." He looked at her head-on. "I could see what was coming for me every time I looked at my caddy."

"Wasn't your father your caddy?" she asked. Too late she began to remember bits and pieces of gossip she'd heard Jack and his golfing buddies chew over about the elder Lashman's blow-ups while Eric had still been on the circuit and she'd still cared enough about her ex-husband to pay attention to his conversation.

"From my first junior tournament. He was also an alcoholic. I grew up thinking it was okay to drink on the job." His mouth curled up at the corners, but it was less a smile than a grimace. It all made sense to her now. Eric's father was an alcoholic. He saw the same tendencies in himself. His next words confirmed her theory. "I couldn't handle the stress of the pro circuit without a crutch. Neither could my old man. But I was able to turn my back on what caused my loss of control. He never could. Being a professional golfer was all he ever wanted in life and, when he wasn't good enough to make a living at it, he drank himself to death. It's a horrible way to die."

"I'm sorry," she said. "My father passed away four years ago. I miss him every day still. How long has your father been gone?"

"Two years. We didn't speak from the day I quit playing golf until the day he died."

"I'm sorry for that, as well," she said softly. The thought of being so completely estranged from a parent was foreign to her. She had loved her father deeply. She and her mother were very close, even though they were separated by a thousand miles. She had her sisters, no matter how exasperating they sometimes were, aunts and uncles and a dozen cousins she stayed in touch with, and her nieces and nephews to spoil. Even though she was sometimes lonely since her divorce, she was never truly alone unless she wanted to be. She felt loved and blessed to have family around her. Eric had no one but his brother. It made her sad to think of him being so alone.

They hadn't spoken of anything very personal since they'd awakened that morning, curiously unembarrassed by the intimacies of sharing a very small living space. It hadn't seemed awkward to her to hear the water running as he showered, the toilet flush. It was more as if they were waiting for just the right time, the right opportunity to take their relationship to the next level of trust, and perhaps now it had come. He was sharing his past with her. She needed to be as honest with him.

"I'm sorry, too. But I could never find the courage to make it right with him, because that would have meant I'd have to tell him my fear of ending up like him is the reason I quit golf," he said, swinging the bottle of mineral water between the tips of his long, strong fingers.

She could understand his dilemma. "A no-win situation."

He nodded in reply. "I'll regret it the rest of my life. He was a great guy when he wasn't drinking. He'd go months stone-cold sober when my brother and I were growing up, but something always made him fall off the wagon. Sometimes it was because he didn't make the cut in a tournament or lost a sponsor. He always took rejection hard, especially after our mother died. She kept him anchored, kept him focused. With her gone, there was no buffer. My brother and I lived in dread of the signs he'd started up again."

And Eric was the big brother. He'd had to grow up fast, take care of all of them. And succeed where his father had failed. He was good at hiding his feelings, but she was a woman and she cared for him. It was easy for her to read his past in the darkness of his gray eyes.

"But you aren't an alcoholic." She didn't make the words a question but she needed to know this about him. Not for an "article" she no longer intended to write, but for her. For them, for what she was beginning to hope they might someday share.

"Not technically, I suppose," he said, looking down at the bottle in his hand for a moment. He lifted his gaze and let her eyes meet his. "But I could be. I might be if I continued to live under the same kind of pressure I did on the tour. That's why I walked away that day at Augusta. I couldn't keep my mind on the putt. Didn't even care that I was heading for a tournament record, that I was leaving all of them, including Tiger Woods, in the dust. All I could think about was getting off the course and having a few drinks. Then I looked up and there was my dad staring back at me. And I saw the exact same thoughts reflected in his eyes. That was it. I just walked away. And I've never looked back."

A cloud moved over the sun. It was quiet in the ancient vineyard, the sounds of the little town muted by the stone wall that hid the two of them from the street. She could hear birds in the trees and insects in the stone pots of flowers grouped around them. The trattoria was deserted this time of day. It catered to the local residents, not tourists, all of whom were home sitting in the shade of their own patios waiting for the cool evening breezes, when they could venture out for dinner and conversation.

A cold fist closed around her heart. He had shared so much with her these last few hours. She must be as honest with him as he had been with her. But how? And when? How could she tell him she had lied about her job? How could she confess that she had cultivated his interest so that she could make a few waves in her very little pond back home with his story, just to ease her own disappointment at being hustled off to the Women's Page? Flawed principles for a woman with small dreams. Is that what he would think of her? The thought filled her with shame and kept her silent once more.

For the first time she let herself admit how limited her prospects were. Was her goal in life to write about high-school sports and small college athletic scandals for the rest of her life when there was so much more world out there to see? She and her sisters had planned this cruise to help her mother break through the boundaries of her prolonged grief. But were its liberating effects working on her, as well? Or did her sudden rest-

lessness have more to do with the handsome, complicated man beside her?

Eric set his empty bottle down on the table and stood
up. He held out his hand and she laid her palm against
his, bracing herself for the jolt of awareness she'd come
to expect with his touch. His fingers curled around hers
and he tugged her gently to her feet. "We should be getting back. Are you ready to leave?"

She picked up Bonnie's camera. Should she take one
more picture of this idyllic place, one with Eric in the
frame so she would have it to remember him by when
she was back in her condo in Dayton? One bright spot
of Mediterranean color in her almost empty white-on-
white living room.

Or her equally barren bedroom.

No, that would be too cruel—to contemplate his
handsome face and sexy body as she crawled into her
empty bed every night. But then she weakened. Better
a bittersweet memory than no memories, at all.

"One more picture," she said, framing him in the
screen against a backdrop of blue sea and flaming red
bougainvillea. "That's a good one," she said, looking at
the still that came up on the small screen.

"Let me see." He peered over her shoulder, shield-
ing the viewer from the sun with one big hand. Heat
poured through Lola's lower body as he brushed against
her, strong and hard.

"Not bad," he said casually.

"Not bad? It's perfectly composed," she retorted,
fighting to regain her equilibrium by taking the offen-
sive. "You're a good subject."

"You get used to the camera in the business I was in,"
he said dismissively.

"Easy for you to say. I always look like a cardboard cut-out, or worse yet, I'm putting food in my mouth. That's my mother's favorite pose for me and my sisters."

He laughed and lifted his hands as though to fend off an attack. "I've never seen a picture of you," he reminded her. "How can I judge?"

She gave the image one more glance. She wondered if it were possible for the man to take a bad picture. Even with the otherworldly beauty of the background and the riot of gaudy flowers around him he was still the object that drew the eye, the focal point, the center of the universe—

The center of the universe? Letting herself think of him in that context was a very bad sign. Time to slow down and get her hormones and her imagination back under control. She began scrolling backward through the morning's pictures. "I'll probably have to go all the way back to Rome to show you what I'm talking about," she explained, hoping her internal upheaval wasn't reflected in her voice. "Unless you managed to sneak in some candid shots of me." It was amazing how easily they fell into a bantering mood. Her relationship with Jack had always been too intense, too fraught with tension to allow them to tease each other without darker undercurrents swimming to the surface.

"Not me," he said. "You haven't let that camera out of your sight for five—" He broke off suddenly. She had arrived at the pictures she had taken in the immediate aftermath of the bombing at Rene's clubhouse. He reached over and took the camera from her. "These are good, Lola," he said. "Powerful. You've got talent."

"I don't know about that," she said, watching the

shots flicker across the small screen with him. "It's hard not to take a good picture with a camera like this."

"Don't dismiss your talent so cavalierly," he said, and this time he wasn't teasing. A picture of the little waitress, Lily, came up. She was crying, surrounded by her coworkers, all of them looking scared and shocked, but doing their best to give comfort to the weakest among them.

"Terrorism," she said quietly. "It's the only time I've experienced it firsthand, and it was terrifying. Even with all the things that have happened in the world these last few years, it's not something that's always on your mind in Dayton, Ohio, you know. You expect it to happen in the big cities, in the Middle East, not…home. And not when you're sitting on a country-club terrace drinking lemonade and admiring the view."

"You should write about what you experienced yesterday for the people back in Dayton. You can preach security from every rooftop, but until it hits home, no one's prepared. You were on a golf outing on a cruise, for God's sake, not sitting on top of the Empire State Building or Big Ben, waiting for a bomb to go off. They should be reminded terrorism isn't an abstract concept. Middle America could be next. They could be next." He was right. Her pictures were good. They would make a powerful statement with the right words to accompany them. Nothing preachy or pedantic, just the facts and her reaction to them. She could write that story.

"We should get these pictures to your editor," he said, his tone giving her no room to argue. "There's an Internet café down the street from the apartment. We can be there in half an hour."

"ARE YOU SURE you wouldn't like to stop for one more gelato?" he asked. The boat from the restaurant had dropped them off at the marina in the middle of the town. They'd taken one of the little orange buses that ran in a circle on the lower streets to the first of the three steep staircases leading back to the apartment.

"I couldn't eat another bite," she said, only a little breathless. She had both her hands wrapped around his arm to steady herself on the steep incline. She'd had two glasses of wine and a tiny aperitif glass of the restaurant's homemade limoncello. She was a long way from drunk, just nicely tipsy, the way you should be after a delicious meal and a long day in the sun and wind.

He liked the fact that she hadn't made a big deal of his not drinking, or that he used to drink too much. She didn't scold. She didn't alter her own habits, as though he hadn't enough self-control to keep from falling off his own particular form of the wagon just because she had a second glass of wine with her fish.

He was finding there wasn't much about Lola Sandler that he didn't like.

And tonight he would have her all to himself again. And this time he intended to do something about it.

"If you don't want a gelato," he said as they climbed past a tiny café with two tables in front of its lighted window, "would you like an espresso?" If she was tipsy that would sober her up. He didn't want it said he'd taken advantage, even the slightest advantage, of her condition.

"No, thanks. I'd be awake all night if I drank that stuff this late. No one in Dayton waits until ten o'clock at night to eat dinner." As though to underscore her words the church bells began to peal the hour. Twelve strokes in what seemed to be as many different bell voices.

"Midnight," she murmured. "The witching hour. And time for this Ohio girl to be in her bed."

Eric felt himself harden at the mere thought of her in bed, because that mundane image led to others, far less innocent, of the two of them together in that bed. "We're here," he said unnecessarily, fishing in his pants' pocket for the big old-fashioned key that opened the street-level door to the apartment's enclosed staircase.

"Thank goodness these are the last," she said, starting up the narrow flight. "I'm tired of climbing steps. I doubt anyone in this town needs a personal trainer. Every time you leave your house it's like one big Stair-Master session."

"I never thought of it that way," he said with a grin. He liked her sharp, quirky sense of humor, too.

She let go of his arm to climb and there was just enough light from the single bulb at the top to treat him to the sight of her gently swaying hips and rounded bottom beneath the thin skirt of her dress. Her scent floated back to him, the herbal soap they'd shared in the bathroom, and some kind of lemony shampoo and, beneath it all, the scent of warm skin…and soft, sexy woman. He'd been hard before. Now he was rigid. Damn, he didn't want her to see him like this…not yet, anyway, he thought ruefully.

He opened the door at the top of the stairs and they walked through the tiny galley kitchen in the dark. She headed straight for the balcony, kicking off her sandals as she went. She leaned her hands on the railing and looked down into the dark, narrow street. "I love this place. I'll be sorry to leave tomorrow." She giggled a little. "Listen to me. I'm exchanging this for an incredible cruise ship, not a cold-water walk-up in Dayton. Am I getting spoiled or what?"

"You're just falling under Italy's spell," he said quietly, coming up behind her but staying far enough away that he could resist the urge to reach out and gather her in his arms. He was falling under her spell for certain, and he had the notion there might not be a counterspell to her magic in this world or any other.

"Mmm," she said, looking up at the heavens. "So many stars even with the town's lights obscuring some of them." She changed the subject with her next breath. "Mom and my sisters will be visiting Pompeii and Herculaneum tomorrow."

"So can we," he said, reaching both hands around her and turning her into his arms. "If we leave here early enough we can be there when the site opens, take our tour and be back at the ship in enough time that it won't look as if I'm trying to con them out of another day's pay."

"I'd like that. I read all about Pompeii when I was a little girl. I'd hate to be so close and miss it."

"We'll have to be up at dawn," he warned. He wanted to sleep beside her, watch her wake up when the sun came through the window and warmed her face.

"I think I can manage that if we go to bed right now." He felt her stiffen as she realized what she'd just said. "I mean—" She stumbled to a halt. Even in the shadows that surrounded them he could see her blush.

"I know what you mean." He pulled her closer and she didn't resist. "My mind's running on the same track. I don't want to sleep on the chaise tonight, Lola. Do you understand what I'm asking you?"

She nodded, a barely perceptible movement of her

head. She dropped her gaze to the level of his chin. "You want to make love to me." Her hair was loose, pushed behind her ears, but one wayward curl had fallen forward against her cheek. He reached out and pushed it behind her ear, following the shell-like curve with the tips of his fingers.

"Very much," he admitted, and realized his own voice was rough with nerves and desire. He wanted her more than he'd ever wanted a woman. But in a subtly different way. He didn't want just her body, although he burned with the need to bury himself inside her heat and softness. He'd always tried to be honest with himself and tonight was no exception. He was pretty sure he was falling in love with her, and the admission amazed and scared him.

But if he told her that, she'd probably run screaming into the night. It was too early for declarations of love. He was getting ahead of himself. He didn't want a one-night stand. He didn't want a shipboard affair. He wanted all of her: Her quirky sense of humor, her toughness, her compassion. And not for just one night, but for as far into the future as he dared to look. This was a tough, tricky course. He needed to play it slow. One swing at a time.

Then Lola raised her eyes to his and met his gaze head-on, and he was lost. Any half-formed strategy he had for a seduction flew out of his head. She lifted her arms and put them around his neck, pulling his mouth down to hers. "I want to kiss you, too," she said on a sigh. "I've wanted to all day long."

CHAPTER SEVENTEEN

IN THE END it had been easy, after all. She just had to stop thinking and let herself feel. Once she had wrapped her arms around his neck and felt his lips on hers, there had been no turning back. From kisses to caresses had taken only moments, or perhaps it was hours, she couldn't remember; time had ceased to flow in an orderly fashion for the whole of the night.

They had moved from the terrace to the bed, items of clothing seeming to shed themselves of their own accord. They made love in the dark, with only the star shine and the light of a waning moon to show them the way. Eric was a good lover. He had moved at her pace, kissed and stroked and carried her beyond the awkwardness of a first encounter. He had been patient, coaxing her past the inhibitions and feelings of inadequacy left behind after her divorce, feelings she'd barely acknowledged to herself, but was now so happy to discard.

Her first climax had taken her unaware, leaving her pliant and sated and filled with feminine triumph as Eric gained his own release with a strangled groan. She dozed off, only to waken to his exploring hands and lips and the same mutual and explosive completion before they both drifted off to sleep at dawn.

Lola awakened from a deep dreamless sleep to find the sun climbing high in the sky. "We're not going to have time to visit Pompeii after all," she said, not quite as disappointed as she thought she'd be. She'd wakened in Eric's arms, her face pressed against his shoulder, her breasts pleasantly abraded by the crisp, wiry hair on his chest as he held her close.

"If we leave right now we can probably hit the high spots," he said, nuzzling her neck, then nibbling at the pearl stud in her ear. Her stomach tightened as she imagined his strong white teeth teasing her nipple in just the same way. She could feel them harden as the image invaded her thoughts, and so did he, because he immediately turned her in his arms and began a slow delicious exploration of both her breasts, while at the same time his hand slipped lower to repeat the delightful caress between her legs.

"And, if we don't?" she asked, wondering why in the world she needed to see a place of death like Pompeii when it was so much better to be alive and making love to a handsome, virile man.

"We can finish what we've started," he said, easing her onto her back, urging her legs apart. "Shower," he said, the tip of his erection seeking entrance to the center of her. "Together."

"Save water," she agreed. "I'm all for conservation."

"Make love," he murmured, urging her legs farther apart.

"Not again so soon after this," she gasped as he entered her, filling her, stretching her, loving her. "We haven't even... Mmm." She sighed, losing her train of thought as she wrapped her arms around his neck.

"There's always time for making love. We're in Italy, remember? And then we'll drive down the coast and stop at the Villa de Poppae site. She was Nero's second wife. It's a fantastic place. Better than Pompeii." He matched his rhythmic strokes to his words, and she wouldn't have cared if he'd been reciting the multiplication tables as long as he went on talking to her in that fascinating accent, pushing deeper within her with every stroke.

She was busy mulling the possibilities of never leaving this place, this bed, and her eyes popped open in surprise when he almost pulled out.

"I was afraid you'd drifted off," he said, half teasing, half serious.

"I was thinking. But I'm paying attention now." She wrapped her legs around his waist. "Stay with me," she whispered. "I don't care about Poppae's villa, or Pompeii, or any place but being here with you." She flicked her tongue in his ear, behaving in the daring, sexy way she'd always wanted to, but had never had the confidence to—until now.

"You're sure you won't miss Pompeii?" His breathing had quickened, his muscles growing tight as he fought for a few more seconds of control, waiting for her.

"No," she said, arching her back, seeking glory. "Anywhere you take me I'll be happy to go." He smiled in triumph as she climaxed around him. With one last deep thrust he came, and they dropped off the edge of the world together.

Two hours later she was afraid they really would drop off the edge of the earth. The drive down from Naples the day before had been harrowing enough in the dark, but in daylight it was awe-inspiring and absolutely terrifying. The roadway consisted of nothing but hairpin turns, oncoming traffic with no regard for safety, and such magnificent views of the coastline that it was nearly impossible for Lola to keep her eyes on the road.

"Just relax," Eric said, grinning. "I'm a good driver. I'll get us back to Naples in one piece. And the car, too," he said, swerving to avoid a motorcycle that had been parked along the very narrow shoulder and decided to merge back into traffic without the least sign of a turn signal or even a wave of the driver's hand just as they pulled even with it.

"We'll be at the villa in another fifteen minutes or so. Can you last that long? Or should I fish around in my pocket and see if I can come up with a tranquilizer?"

"You take tranquilizers?" she asked, diverted for a moment from scanning the oncoming traffic for suicide drivers.

"No, I don't," he said. "It was a joke."

"Well, I just wondered," she replied, getting in a little zinger of her own. "You managed to come up with half a dozen condoms without batting an eye."

"I have to admit I thought I was being optimistic when I bought them."

"I would have thought you were being delusional if I'd known what you were up to," she confessed, smiling as she watched his grinning profile. She, Lola Sandler, Miss Uptight and Dateless, had made love six times in less than a day. Unbelievable. Unforgettable. She snuggled down into the leather seat to contemplate the reality of it, then grabbed the dashboard with both hands as a minibus full of wide-eyed tourists careened past them at half the speed of light. "Those poor people," she said.

He laughed, and she fell just a little bit further in love with him.

The thought brought her up short, shocking her heart into a stutter.

She *was* falling in love with him. How could that be? They barely knew each other. Surely, it was only lust. Surely, it wasn't the *for sure, real thing,* as Alex liked to say.

Eric took his hand off the steering wheel and folded hers inside. "Relax," he said. He was watching her from behind the mirrored lenses of his sunglasses. She could feel the focused intensity of his gaze even though she couldn't see his eyes. "Enjoy yourself. Let me take care of you for today."

Take care of her. She thought of all the ways he could mean the phrase and couldn't find one of them to object to. Oh, yes, she thought, bowing to the inevitable. It was the for sure, real thing.

She turned her hand in his so that their fingers intertwined for just a moment before he returned both hands to the wheel. "Today, I'm all yours."

"AND THAT'S EVERYTHING that's happened from the time I left the ship in Corsica until right now," Lola said, curling one leg under her as she leaned back against the padded banquette in La Belle Epoque, her mother's favorite spot on the ship for after-dinner drinks and dancing with Señor Mendoza.

Bonnie and Frances sat on the other side of the table,

drinks in hand, and said, "Uh-huh" in the same skeptical tone of voice.

"Do you expect us to believe you were alone with a hunk like Eric Lashman for two nights running and nothing happened?" Bonnie asked, disbelief tingeing her words.

"Lola, I thought you'd give us more credit than that," Frances declared in her best principal's voice. "Mom might have bought your 'he slept on the chaise on the balcony' explanation, but I changed almost as many of your diapers as she did, and I deal with thirteen-year-olds trying to lie their way out of trouble every day. I know when you're not telling the truth."

Lola felt warm all over. She hoped the low lighting hid her blush. She'd never been good at keeping secrets from her big sisters. They simply knew her too well. But she was almost thirty years old and there was a first time for everything. "I'm not going to discuss my love life in a public place," she said, mustering her dignity.

"Why not? No one's paying any attention to us." Bonnie leaned forward eagerly. She was smiling and there was a teasing lilt in her voice. "C'mon, Lola Roly-Pola, something happened. You've got stars in your eyes."

Something had happened to her troubled sister over the two days they'd been separated. All the tension had drained out of her. She seemed relaxed and at peace with herself. She'd made up her mind about the baby, Lola surmised, and was content with the choice she had made. But what decision had she come to? There hadn't been time for any private conversation among the sisters since she'd reboarded *Alexandra's Dream*.

Myra and Bonnie and Frances's shore excursion to Pompeii hadn't returned to the ship until it was time to dress for dinner. Lola had taken the opportunity to dress early, and once the hugs and kisses and demands to be assured she wasn't hurt were answered to everyone's satisfaction, she'd slipped out of the cabin and gone up on deck, grateful to postpone the interrogation that was sure to come.

"I don't have stars in my eyes," Lola retorted, forcing her thoughts away from memories of Positano and the Amalfi coast. "It's just the reflections from the lights on the dance floor. And speaking of the dance floor," she said, attempting to deflect her sisters' single-minded intent to ferret out every intimate detail of her time with Eric, "aren't Mom and Señor Mendoza breaking the rules again? I know this is their third dance."

Bonnie turned her head to look out at the dance floor but Fran's unwavering gaze remained fixed on Lola. "You're not going to wiggle out of this so easily," she said.

Bonnie settled back in her seat. "She doesn't know," she said with a grin. "Mom didn't say anything at dinner so she doesn't know."

"Doesn't know what?" Her ploy had worked, at least for the moment, but Lola wasn't sure she wanted to hear what Bonnie was so eager to tell.

"It doesn't matter how many times Antonio dances with Mom, anymore."

"Antonio?" Her sister was calling the man by his first name now?

"It happened right here," Fran explained. "After we knew you were all right and that you would meet us here today. Mom and Señor Mendoza were dancing."

"Slooowww dancing," Bonnie broke in, rolling her eyes. "The ship's hotel manager must have been watching, because when Antonio brought Mom back to our table, he just appeared out of nowhere and asked Antonio to please accompany him to his office."

Fran took over the story at that point. "Señor Mendoza declined to leave the dance floor. He said he intended to dance with Mom as often as she would partner him."

"And then he gave her one of those little bows he's so good at. Like she was a queen and he was her champion."

Fran frowned at the interruption.

"Sorry," Bonnie murmured with another grin.

"The hotel manager said that he regretted it, but he would have to terminate his contract, and he would be charged for his passage and never allowed to be a gentleman host for Liberty Line again," Fran concluded with a dramatic flourish.

"Then what happened?" Lola asked. Evidently, she wasn't the only member of the family indulging in a romantic adventure over the last two days.

"Antonio took out his wallet, pulled out a platinum credit card—and it wasn't the only one I saw in there," Bonnie confided in a whisper. "And told the hotel manager to have his things moved to the penthouse suite!" She leaned back in her chair, clapping her hands and laughing. "It was even better than one of Grandma Hilver's romance novels."

"Evidently he *is* from a rich sherry-producing family," Fran said. "And he was just on the cruise because he was lonely and he loves to dance. He's not a gigolo or out to get Mom's money."

"Although, I'm pretty sure he's out to get Mom," Bonnie added.

"You're kidding, right?" Lola shot her mother and the distinguished Spaniard another glance. They were wrapped in each other's arms, oblivious to the rest of the couples on the dance floor.

Bonnie crossed her heart just as she'd done when Lola was a little girl and she wanted to be assured her big sister was telling her the truth. "Every word is true. Even the part about the penthouse suite. Mom was up there. She says it's gorgeous. There's a butler and a grand piano and everything."

"Is she... Is she in love with him?" Lola felt as if the whole world had just tilted a little off center. She curled her hands around the edge of the seat, hoping everything would right itself before she got sick to her stomach.

"She hasn't confided in us," Fran admitted. "Would it be so awful if she did fall in love with Señor Mendoza? He seems like a nice man. She's been so lonely since Dad died. She deserves someone. And he could certainly show her a good time."

"I—I don't know," Lola said truthfully. "I'll have to think about it."

"We all do," Bonnie said. "I'll miss her so much if she moves away. I'm so spoiled having her nearby."

Move away? To Spain? Lola hadn't considered that possibility, either.

She stood up. "I've got to go," she said. "I need to get this all straight in my head. Tell Mom... Just tell her something for me, okay?"

"We'll cover for you, but you're not going off just to contemplate the possibility of a rich, Spanish stepfather," Bonnie said knowingly. "You're going off to meet Eric Lashman. Don't think we've forgotten about you two just because you sidetracked us into talking about Mom and Antonio."

Lola didn't even acknowledge her sister's last salvo,

just waved a distracted goodbye as she hurried out of the nightclub, across the corridor and into the nearest elevator.

Could it be that her mother had found love on the cruise? Was it possible to fall in love with someone in the space of a handful of days?

Was that what was happening to her? Is that why she was so anxious to find Eric and talk with him? Touch him. Make love with him again? Was she that far gone, already, that a few hours apart from him seemed like days?

She hadn't been consciously moving in any one direction, or so she thought, until she emerged on the sports deck and found it empty of his presence. The disappointment was almost a physical pain. Where was he? Had he only been delayed? Or had he forgotten their hurried plans to meet here at midnight when they parted after their return to the ship?

She looked at her watch: 12:08 p.m. The sports deck was deserted except for a couple strolling hand in hand toward the observation platform and a lone runner on the treadmill in the health club. Through the window she could see the large digital clock hung on the wall. The numerals read 12:11 p.m. Had he stood her up? Had last night really been just a one-night stand? Her *Affair to Remember* and nothing more?

CHAPTER EIGHTEEN

"LOLA." She was standing with her back to him, staring out at the lights of Naples. She turned at the sound of his voice, her expression slightly wistful, as though she were feeling a little sad and lost. Then her eyes met his and a smile tugged at the corners of her mouth, growing to wreath her face and light fires in her green eyes.

"I thought you stood me up," she said as he covered the last few yards of teak decking between them. She was wearing a short swingy dress in all the shades of a fiery sunset. Her hair was pulled up on top of her head and held in place with a handful of sparkly little combs. She didn't throw her arms around his neck, or rush into his arms, but turned back to watch the longshoremen loading provisions into the ship's hold seventy-five feet below. A cruise ship like *Alexandra's Dream* took on fresh food and supplies at almost every port it visited.

"I'm only five minutes late," he said.

"Eight," she corrected him, turning slightly so that she faced him more directly. "Not that I'm keeping track of the time or anything like that."

He covered her hand with his, angling his body to shield them from any strolling passersby or fitness nuts walking the treadmills in the gym. "Well, I was. I couldn't get away from Father Connelly. He cornered me in the atrium and asked if I'd seen Ariana Bennett anytime today."

"Ariana Bennett?"

"She's the ship's librarian."

Lola nodded. "I've met her. Is she missing?"

"I don't know. No one's raised the alarm if she is. The priest was looking for her, just wanted to know if I'd seen her. Don't know what it's about."

"Well, I haven't seen her, either. I've been in La Belle Epoque with my mother and sisters all evening. What have you been doing besides talking to the good Father?"

"Lying low for my brother's sake," he said.

She tilted her head to study his face. "You sound a little testy," she said.

He'd thought it didn't show. She was learning to read him too well. He sifted through his thoughts to see how he felt about that further sign of growing intimacy and decided it was fine.

"I'm not exactly tops in Nick Pappas's book as you might have noticed when we came aboard." He let a grin gain a foothold at the corners of his mouth. "Thanks for coming to my rescue. You might have saved my brother's job for him."

The master of *Alexandra's Dream* had met them in the Liberty Plaza, the ship's main lobby, alerted by security, most likely. He had greeted Lola warmly, but formally, inquiring after her health and conveying his regrets that he could not hold the ship for her in Ajaccio.

She had given the tall Greek one of her toe-curling smiles and told him she understood completely, that the safety of his ship and her passengers and crew must always come first. She'd thanked him just as prettily for allowing her mother to send her passport on shore with the pilot boat so that she was saved the further trauma, not to mention the expenditure in time and money, of having to secure a new passport in Marseilles.

Nick Pappas had unbent enough to return her smile with one of his own. But when he'd turned his dark gaze on Eric, his face had been once more stern. He'd welcomed him back with no real enthusiasm, asked if he needed the ship's doctor to look at the injuries he'd sustained in the blast and if they would impede the performance of his duties for the remainder of the time he was on board his ship. There had been a decided chill in his words when he'd delivered that final statement. Eric got the impression that one more infraction, no matter how minor, would result in his being escorted off the ship. He began to wonder how he'd break the news to his brother that he'd gotten not only himself but Andrew fired from his job?

That was when Lola had gone into action, describing the bombing in great detail, going so far as to couple the word *hero* with his name once or twice, painting a word picture that even had Eric wondering what would come next.

Nick Pappas had met his match and knew it. Once more he'd voiced his happiness that Lola and Eric were safe and back on board *Alexandra's Dream,* begged her to pass on his compliments to her mother and sisters and, with a brief nod of dismissal to Eric, marched off to return to his duties on the bridge.

"Captain Pappas had no business blaming you for what happened," Lola said with patently false sincerity. "I merely described the events to him as I remembered them."

"You should be writing fiction then, instead of editing the Woman's Page," he said, finding it harder and harder not to sweep her up in his arms and carry her down to his small but surprisingly cheery cabin on the lowest passenger deck. He hadn't been able to stop thinking about their lovemaking, the way she felt in his arms, the way she moved beneath him. The way she'd touched his heart.

Her smile faded. She turned a little away from him. "Don't make me out to be something I'm not. I was only telling the truth. You were a hero. Rene might have bled to death if you hadn't been there to help. LeSatz was only interested in his men and that horrible minister-of-whatever flew off and left us all there. The chef was concerned with Lily and the rest of the staff—"

This time he listened to his instincts. "Okay, okay. It was a compliment, Lola, not a condemnation."

"I'm just good at telling stories, that's all."

"That's not all you're good at," he said, and was rewarded with a wash of color rising in her throat and cheeks.

"Shh, someone will hear you."

"And someone will see us." He lowered his mouth to hers, wondering what he had said to upset her. She was upset; he could feel her trembling in his arms. But as his lips played over hers, the trembling ceased. He could sense her warming to him as her mouth opened to his. A shiver of delight ran through her when his tongue invaded the sweetness of her mouth and the kiss grew deeper.

Her hands came up and clutched the lapels of his jacket. She leaned a little into him and he could feel the tips of her breasts through the thin fabric of her dress and his shirt. He raised his hand to cradle the back of her head. Her hair was as silky as her dress.

"I want to take you to bed again," he murmured against her throat as he reluctantly broke off the kiss. "But I can't. It's against regulations for cruise-line employees to have overnight guests in their cabins. I can't take the chance of further jeopardizing my brother's job."

"I don't think it's a good idea, anyway," she said, reaching up to smooth her fingertips along his temple. "I don't think very clearly when you're lying naked beside me, and we need to consider the consequences this time."

The image her words evoked made him harder than ever. He laid his forehead against hers. "If you keep talking like that, it's not going to matter what either one of us thinks is for the best. It's just going to happen, a force of nature like an earthquake or a hurricane in Florida."

"No, it's not. We're not kids. We can control our appetites."

His appetites maybe, but his emotions were beginning to get the better of him. He didn't want her pulling back this way. He wanted her the way she'd been this morning, passionate and giving. *His.* "Lola, what's wrong? Do you regret what we shared?"

"No," she said emphatically. "No regrets."

"Then what's wrong?"

"Where are we going, Eric? I don't indulge in one-night stands, but maybe it's better to break that rule this once than to have a shipboard romance that ends up breaking my heart." She pulled her hands from beneath his. "It was beautiful, Eric, wonderful. But maybe it should end here and now." She looked so serious, and there was a sheen of tears in her eyes that tugged at his heart. "My mother and sisters are already suspicious."

"You haven't told them about us?"

She stepped back, putting a few inches of between them. A night breeze swirled across the deck, cooling his heated skin, bringing the sounds of music and laughter, reminding him they weren't alone.

"What is there to tell?" she asked. "That we had a night of fantastic sex, but that was probably all there was to it? I don't want to tarnish my memories by having the people I love think I was foolish enough to lose my head and jump into bed with the golf pro."

That angered him. He reached down and circled her wrist with his hand before she could pull away. "It wasn't a fling. Or a one-night stand. It's not a shipboard romance, either," he growled, anticipating her next argument. "It's going to last a hell of a lot longer than a ten-day cruise. Do you understand me?"

Her eyes widened in surprise. "What are you saying?"

"I'm saying I'm this bloody close to falling in love with you." He put his thumb and index finger together and wiggled it in her face. "And I'll bet my last dollar you're just as close to falling in love with me but you won't admit it." He jerked her close, uncaring if there were others watching. He couldn't let her go. Couldn't let her walk out of his life without telling her how he felt. "I know the timing isn't great. I've got to stay on this bloody ship until my brother can get back on board. I might have to go to Corsica again before I can get back to the States, but I'm asking you to wait for me. Don't tell me it's over between us, Lola." He folded her into his embrace, kissed the top of her head, then her eyelids and finally her lips. "Give me a chance to make you fall in love with me completely and forever."

"HE KISSED ME AGAIN until I saw stars and fireworks and couldn't get my breath, and then he turned on his heel and walked away."

"And you went after him, right? Told him you'd follow him to the ends of the earth." Bonnie dropped onto her pillows, her hand on her heart. "Tell me you didn't let him get away."

"In point of fact I didn't do any such thing. I came back here."

Bonnie sat up, then flopped back on the bed. "I can't believe you were so stupid," she said bluntly. Lola had walked back to their cabin in a daze, only to find her sisters there before her, getting ready for bed. "The man all but proposed to you and you didn't say yes?"

"He didn't all but propose. He said he wanted to see me when he gets to the States."

"Then he kissed you into a near catatonic state and walked away without an answer?" Lola looked up in time to see the frown on her oldest sister's face. "Why?"

"Possibly because I didn't give him one. I don't know what to do." Lola knew she sounded miserable. "He still thinks I'm the Women's Page editor—and that I always have been," she said, holding up a restraining hand when she saw Bonnie open her mouth to refute her statement. "I feel like such a sorry excuse for a human being. He's been so honest with me about his life and I've been lying to him about myself ever since we met."

"It's more of an omission than a lie," Fran said, watching Lola's reflection in the mirror of the vanity table where she was sitting, taking off her makeup.

"He's an honorable man. He'll think it's a lie. And it isn't even so much that I haven't told him I'm a sports reporter and plan to be again someday—" oddly enough she couldn't muster as much indignation over her job situation as she had just days before "—it's that sooner or later he's going to ask me what it was that attracted me to him and then what do I say? I figured out who you were and I thought an interview with the elusive and mysterious Eric Lashman would get me my job on the sports desk back?"

Bonnie let out a gusty sigh. "That's exactly what you'll say." She threw out her arms as though offering herself up for a sacrifice. "And ruin everything. For once in your life, don't tell the truth, Lola Roly-Pola. Really, I mean it. Lie through your teeth. Tell him you had the hots for him the moment you saw him."

Lola managed a rueful smile. "Well, that's not entirely false."

"Good, you are normal, after all. I was afraid after being married to that Neanderthal, Jack, that you'd gone over to the other side or something." She grinned. "Not that there's anything wrong with that."

"Bonnie's right," Frances agreed. "Go with your heart and don't borrow trouble." She stood up from the dressing table. "And the sooner the better. Call his cabin and tell him you'll meet him for breakfast."

"I can't." Lola fended off Bonnie's sputtering protest with a wave of her hand. "He's got a group going for a nine-hole outing first thing in the morning."

"Who in their right mind would brave Naples' rush-hour traffic for nine holes of golf?" Frances said from the bathroom, where she'd gone to wash her face. She stepped back into the room with a towel still in her hand. "It's sheer madness, not to mention dumb when there's so much to see and do in this city."

"And the ship sails at two, so they won't have time to see any of the sights. But that will give you time to have a late lunch with Eric. Go ahead—call him." Bonnie rolled onto her side and gestured to the house phone.

Lola shook her head. "I'll see him tomorrow. Maybe by then I'll have everything I want to say worked out in my mind."

"Don't overthink it," her sister cautioned. "It will only cause you heartache. I know, believe me." She placed her hand on her stomach, exchanged glances with Frances and then smiled up at Lola. "Tad and I have worked it out. About the baby. You don't have to worry about me anymore. There's going to be another mouth to feed in the Kanine house."

Lola dropped to her knees beside Bonnie's bed and gave her sister a hug. "I'm so glad. What happened? What changed your mind?"

"My big hunk of a husband—and this little 'oops' did," Bonnie said, laying her hand on her stomach. "I didn't have a chance to tell you before this because I still don't want Mom to know what I was contemplating." She shrugged and gave a little chagrined laugh. "Okay, okay. I see your point about Eric and the interview ploy—"

"Don't worry about me and Eric. What did Tad say that changed your mind?"

"Well, first, he threatened to get the next plane out of Tampa and hunt me down and drag me home so that we could settle this in our own home. In our own bed.

And then I started crying and saying, 'See, that's why I'm so worried. How can you afford to do a crazy thing like that?' And then he started crying. And Tad never cries! Except at Daddy's funeral—" Bonnie's gray eyes filled with tears at the memory.

"You're getting off track," Fran said briskly, patting Bonnie's leg as she sat down on the foot of her bed, but when Lola looked at her oldest sister, she saw the gleam of tears in her eyes.

Bonnie took a deep breath. "He was crying. I was crying. He said he loved me. *And the baby moved.*" She crossed her heart. "I swear to you I felt the baby move. I know you're going to say it's too early to feel it move. I'm only eleven weeks along. But I know it was the baby. He recognized his daddy's voice. I'm positive that's what it was. And then it was just all so clear." She gripped Lola's hand between her own and squeezed. "We'll manage. Together. We'll make room for this baby and love him and worry over him and bless ourselves every day we live. And I was a complete idiot ever to think it could be otherwise."

Lola didn't try to hide her tears. "I'm so glad," she said. "So very happy for you." She laid the tips of her fingers on her sister's belly. "You're a lucky little guy, you know that? You've got the best mommy and daddy in the world."

"And the best aunts." Bonnie reached out and gave Lola a hug. "Now it's late and we've still got a lot of sightseeing to do tomorrow. Capodimonte," she said, lying back with a blissful sigh. "I have to see the Porcelain Gallery, and where they make nativity scenes. Naples is famous for their *presepio*. That's what they're called here. Fran's not the only one who can read a guidebook." She yawned sleepily.

"I'm turning the lights out now," Fran announced, taking charge of the three of them as she always had. Lola didn't mind. She was too relieved to care who was bossing her around tonight.

"How about you and Gary? Did I miss some big meeting of the minds for you two while I was stranded on Corsica?"

Fran straightened from turning down her sheets. The cabin was almost dark, only the night light in the bathroom shone through the open doorway, holding back the darkness. "No breakthroughs," she said, but she didn't sound too upset. "We've been e-mailing. We'll work out something for the boys' sake. We always do. That's why we've managed to stay happily divorced all these years."

"And that's the way you want it to stay?" Lola asked, climbing the narrow ladder into her berth.

"That's the way it's best for us," Fran said. She reached over and straightened Lola's blanket just as she'd done when she was little and Fran was babysitting her so their parents could have a night out. "Don't let what happened to your marriage to Jack scare you off from trying again with Eric. He's a great guy even if we've only known him a short time. Quality shows. Promise?"

"Promise me, too," Bonnie said from below, her voice already heavy with sleep.

"I promise," Lola said. "Now everyone go to sleep. Naples is also known for its pastries and I want to try every single kind." Bonnie was right. She was tired and tomorrow would be a long eventful day. Would she have the courage to go to Eric and offer to share her life with him? At the moment the thought scared her to death, but when she let herself think of her future with him by her side, the fear receded and happiness took its place.

Bonnie and Fran were probably right. She was attaching too much importance to the situation with her job. They'd known each other less than a week, after all. Everything had happened so quickly in their relationship, it wasn't surprising they'd skipped a step or two in communicating. But tomorrow she would set everything right. Tomorrow would be the first day of the rest of her life.

She smiled to herself. One of the oldest clichés in the book—in journalism, something to be avoided. But sometimes clichés really did say it best.

CHAPTER NINETEEN

"I THOUGHT THE TRAFFIC in Rome was terrifying, but that was before I saw how they drive in Naples," Myra said, clinging to Antonio's arm as they maneuvered their way off the double-decker sightseeing bus that had deposited them within walking distance of the ship. They had spent the morning "doing" Naples, and Bonnie had a sack of Bubble-Wrapped and astonishingly ugly examples of porcelain flowers in unnatural colors to prove it.

"Look, there's a *pasticceria*. Want to stop for something sweet? They serve gelato, too. This will be your last chance to get some, Lola." Frances gestured toward the small café, guidebook in hand.

"I suppose I can force down one more serving," Lola said with a grin.

"My youngest daughter has become a gelato junkie on this cruise," Myra said, smiling up at her companion. "Luckily for her, she takes after my husband's family. Every bite of sweets I take ends up on my hips."

"You look lovely just as you are, *mi corazón*," Antonio said gallantly, and, Lola had to admit, with sincerity. "I wouldn't change a thing about you."

Her mother laughed and patted his cheek. "You are so good for me, Antonio."

"When you all come to visit me in Spain, I will show you where there are many good places to eat," he said, turning on the charm for Lola and her sisters.

"I've always wanted to visit Spain," Frances said. "Thanks for the invitation."

"Antonio's home is three-hundred years old," Myra confided. "I can't wait to see it."

Her mother might end up living in Spain—at least, part of the time—if she and Antonio's affair grew more serious. Lola didn't know how she felt about that.

She didn't know how she felt about anything today except that she was anxious and antsy to get back aboard *Alexandra's Dream* and talk to Eric. She was going to tell him everything about herself that she'd been holding back, from the truth about her situation at the *Sentinel* to the fact that she'd sought him out in hopes of getting an interview. Regardless of what Bonnie'd said about keeping that fact to herself, she felt she owed Eric total honesty from this point forward in their relationship.

They took their seats at the outdoor café they had chosen and gave their orders for gelato and pastries and, at Antonio's suggestion, some of the medallions of dark chocolate with liqueur centers called *ministeriale,* for which the city was famous. Naples was a busy, noisy city, somewhat offputting after the relative quiet of Amalfi and Positano. Traffic noises precluded any real conversation, but Lola caught snatches of Bonnie and Myra's conversation about living in the danger zone surrounding Mt. Vesuvius, and how it seemed not to bother anyone in the area. Villages and vineyards were scattered all around and even on the slopes of the volcano itself.

"It's not much different from living in Florida, I guess," Bonnie concluded, relaxing back in her seat. "You never know when a hurricane or a tornado is going to pick you up and blow you out to sea."

Their food arrived then and everyone was occupied for several minutes with tasting and sharing the sweet delights. Lola turned in her seat to accept a spoonful of Bonnie's berry gelato to sample when her attention was caught by a television in a nearby shop window. She watched the large flat screen for several moments before the images displayed there penetrated her consciousness.

"Oh, Lord," she whispered, the spoonful of icy treat still melting on her tongue, "it can't be."

"Can't be, what?' Bonnie swiveled in her seat to follow Lola's riveted gaze. "Lola? Is that you?" She looked at Lola, then turned her head swiftly back to the screen. "It is you. Those are the pictures you took with my camera of the bombing on Corsica, aren't they? How on earth did they get on Italian TV?"

"It's not Italian TV," Lola said, her heart dropping into the pit of her stomach. "It's ESPN. See their logo in the bottom corner of the screen. Somehow ESPN got copies of the pictures I sent to the *Sentinel* from Positano."

By now, all five of them were staring at the big screen, ignoring the food and drink in front of them. Antonio was looking confused but he didn't say anything and, for that, Lola was grateful. A feeling of dread began to grow inside her. They had focused on the picture of Eric working to fashion Rene's splint and froze the image long enough for Lola to realize they were talking about him. She stood up, moved around the low, wrought iron fence that set off the café's tables from the street and walked into the little shop where the TV was displayed.

"Ciao! Posso aiutarti?" the salesclerk said politely.

"No, thanks, we're just looking around," Bonnie responded, having followed Lola into the shop.

Lola could only shake her head. "Please," she said, pointing to the screen. "Is that ESPN?"

"Si," the shaggy-haired young man answered, and then in English, "we have the satellite."

The captioning at the bottom of the screen was in Italian but the announcer was speaking in English, and what he was saying was even worse than Lola had imagined. Somehow they had gotten her pictures of the bombing from her editor, she surmised. It was the only explanation. He must have put the story out over the wire. But it wasn't the images of the golf-course bombing that were so terrible. It was the story that the sports network had added to them.

There were pictures of Eric when he was on the tour. And there were pictures of his father, looking dissipated and ill. Even a shot of Eric and his brother at a funeral. Her heart bled to see the pain on Eric's face as he followed the casket from a stone church to a waiting hearse. And then, in the studio, three ex-jocks behind a curved table asked the question she'd once thought she would be the one to answer: "Where is he now?"

"How often have they shown this story?" she asked.

The salesman looked at the screen and shrugged. "I don't know. Two, maybe three times I have seen it."

"Oh, no." Lola felt like bursting into tears. "This is terrible."

"What?" Bonnie asked, puzzled. "That they used your pictures, or that they dredged up all that stuff from Eric's past? That's not your fault."

"I know. But will Eric feel the same? Oh, hell," she said, not caring who heard her. "I can't believe this is happening. What will I do when he sees this?" She waved her hand at the oversized screen. A new graphic had appeared in black and white, with bold-faced letters impossible to miss: *Corsica photos courtesy of* Dayton Sentinel *Sports Editor, Lola Sandler.*

CHAPTER TWENTY

IT HAD BEEN A LONG DAY. Eric was glad to be back aboard, able to retreat to his small cabin and head into the shower. The day had been hot and sticky, typical weather for Naples at the end of August. The course the dozen diehard duffers he'd shepherded had played was mediocre at best, with only a fantastic view of Mt. Vesuvius to save it from complete obscurity. Southern Italy was not a golfing mecca but his charges hadn't seemed to mind, happily swinging away, heedless of the heat and humidity.

He'd done his best to hide his impatience, mindful of his brother's future with the cruise line, but he couldn't wait to get back, shower, change and find Lola. They had so much to settle between them, and so little time to do it. Tomorrow the ship stopped in Palermo—after that, a day at sea and then Venice. A few hours later Lola would be on her way back to the States. The last night of a cruise was usually an early one, for most passengers, and there were lots of distractions. He wanted to take their relationship to the next level before then if he could manage it.

The next level. Did that mean he just wanted to continue seeing her when he returned to the States?

Or more?

He peeled off his clothes and stepped into the shower, letting the lukewarm water sluice away the sweat and sunblock from his skin. The water pressure was down, he noticed, as it always was when they were in port, but he was used to that. He was also used to the cramped confines of his brother's cabin. At least he didn't have to share, like many of the other employees of the cruise line, although the cabin's location, down a busy corridor from the medical offices, across from the elevators and next to a service area, was less than ideal.

They would have privacy, at least, if not a great deal of comfort, should Lola agree to return here with him tonight. He couldn't ask her to stay, even if she wanted to, because of the stipulations of Andrew's contract, but they could be alone for a while. Long enough for him to propose. And for her to accept?

There. He'd formed the longing into a concrete thought.

He was tired of being alone. He was ready for a partner, ready to settle down.

He was ready to fall in love. He went a step further. He was already in love with Lola Sandler and he wanted to marry her. No alarm bells went off in his brain, no rush of dread. He'd made his decision and he would follow it through just as he always did.

He was committed.

Now he only had to convince Lola she was in love with him, too.

Eric turned off the water and stepped out of the shower stall. He grabbed a towel and rubbed himself dry. When he opened the mirrored cabinet above the sink, he was a little surprised to find his hands were shaking.

He was in love. He'd never been head over heels before, but he liked it. At least, he would when Lola was his. He grinned and wrapped the damp towel around his middle as he walked the three steps to the other side of the cabin and turned on the TV. He would propose to her tonight. It was formal night. He had to wear his bloody tux, anyway. He might as well make use of it. He wondered if she would wear that slinky black number she'd worn the first day they'd met.

Should he buy her flowers? What about a ring? That stopped him short for a moment, but then he decided a ring could wait until they had a chance to pick one out together. He flipped through the channels looking for ESPN. He may not play on the pro tour, anymore, but he was still a man, and any sport played with any size ball, anywhere in the world, beat just about anything else there was to watch.

What he didn't expect to see was his own face staring back at him from the screen. "What the bloody hell?" he asked out loud, toggling up the volume.

A roundtable of ex-jocks in a studio were discussing his damned life and whereabouts, surprised he'd surfaced in such a spectacular manner. Eric sat down hard on the bed, watching in grim fascination as the pictures Lola had taken the day of the bombing at Rene's golf course flashed on the screen, followed by a montage of his career and clips of several of his father's more public escapades, including the mug shot of the older Lashman's drunk-driving arrest in Palm Springs after the Desert Open the year before Eric had left the tour.

He hit the mute button. He didn't need to know what the trio was saying. He'd heard it all before in one form or another. He didn't have to listen, but he couldn't look away. He continued to watch in silence, steeling himself for the one picture he knew was to come. And it did. There it was. The shot of Andrew and him following their dad's casket out of the church. God, that one hurt. It always would. The worst day of his life, knowing he'd let the old man go to his grave without the two of them making peace with each other.

He stood up and tightened the towel around his middle, trying to shrug off the residue of guilt and sadness the images evoked. He wasn't mad at the network. It wouldn't do any good if he was. He was a public figure, or, at least, he had been. He was fair game. He hadn't paid attention to himself on TV for a long time, and he didn't intend to start again. Granted, it was a jolt to the system, got the adrenaline pumping, made him want to take a three iron to the TV screen, but he'd get over it. The story was just a fluke, one last fifteen minutes of fame that would drop out of the news cycle in less than a day.

But who in hell had given the sports network the pictures Lola had taken?

He'd watched her upload the pictures to the *Sentinel* Web site in the little Internet café in Positano. Had her boss put them out on the wire services? Most likely explanation, he supposed, running his hand through his hair. He'd have to have a talk with her. He stood up and reached over his head to turn off the small TV when one last shock stayed his hand. A crawl of words across the bottom of the screen caught his attention. *Corsica photos courtesy of* Dayton Sentinel *Sports Editor, Lola Sandler.*

Sports editor?

He blinked and looked again. Not Women's Page editor. Sports editor.

She'd lied to him about her job. Why? A second question followed on the heels of the first.

What else had she lied to him about?

There was a sharp knock on the door, then another and a third. Distracted by the events of the last few minutes, he covered the short distance to the door and pulled it open without even bothering to put on his robe.

"Lola." He saw her look past his shoulder to the TV, where a shot of him brandishing his putter over his head like a sword after he'd won the Open, was projected behind the talking heads. "What the hell is going on?"

HE LOOKED SO ANGRY Lola almost lost her nerve. She had to swallow twice before she could get any words past the lump in her throat. "You know," she said. It was all she could manage. "I'm sorry. Really sorry. I came to warn you that—"

She broke off suddenly, realizing he was wearing nothing but a damp towel that enhanced, rather than hid, his attributes. His hair was still wet from the shower, and the hair on his chest spangled with water droplets. She couldn't think straight suddenly, as her brain switched from rational to sexual in the space of a heartbeat.

"What the bloody—" He stopped and started over. "What's going on, Lola? Where did those pictures come from?"

"My boss," she said miserably. "It had to have been my boss."

He nodded curtly. Two members of the service staff walked by, giggling behind their hands. Lola saw them giving him the once-over and felt even worse than before. Eric gave the women a dark look. "Come inside," he said in a tone that didn't give her any leeway to argue as he stepped back from the door.

Lola hesitated. The last thing she wanted was to be alone with him in a confined space when he was not only angry with her, but more than half naked. She shook her head. "I'll stay here, it won't take me long to apologize."

"Lola—" now he sounded annoyed "—at least wait for me to get dressed."

"There's really no reason. I'm sorry this happened. I know you treasure your privacy. And those pictures of your father…his funeral." She had to stop talking and swallow the knot of self-disgust that had lodged in her throat.

"To hell with that. You have to have skin like rhino hide to survive on the pro tour. Just because I gave it up doesn't mean I can't still take the hits. But why did you lie to me about being a sports reporter? That is your real job, isn't it? You're not the Women's Page editor."

"I am now—I didn't have a choice," she said, realizing as she'd feared that her explanation was going to sound even weaker spoken out loud than it did in her head. "There was a problem with my ex-husband's basketball team. He coaches women's college basketball. Performance-enhancing drugs."

"Go on." He backed up a couple of steps and hooked a robe from the bathroom door. "I take it your ex was implicated, right?" He shrugged his arms into the sleeves and belted the robe tight around his slim waist.

The constriction in Lola's chest eased just a little. She found she could almost take a normal breath now that she didn't have to stare at his bare chest. "Right. There was a big investigation. The owners of the *Sentinel* are really conservative. They wouldn't stand for a hint of impropriety. I got booted off the story and onto the Women's Page. I—I was angry. It happened just a few months ago." Here was the part she dreaded. The part where his eyes would turn the cold, hard gray of granite and he would tell her to start walking and never look back.

"When I found out who you were, I decided to strike up a friendship to get an exclusive interview and use that for leverage to wheedle my way back into my old job." The excuse sounded sordid even to her own ears. That was not the way she operated. It wasn't the kind of woman she was.

"You used me," he said in a strangled voice. She couldn't look him in the eye any longer.

"Yes, and I'm so sorry. After that night on the sports deck, when we talked about the things we wanted in life, I knew I had to tell you the truth about my job. But things moved so quickly, and then there was the bombing and…"

"Things moved even quicker," he said. She fixed her gaze on the bronzed skin of his throat between the lapels of the robe.

"Yes. And then I knew I wouldn't write the story, ever, because I—I was falling in love with you." He moved a little, as if he might reach out for her, or grab her and shake her; she wasn't sure which. "Please, don't think too badly of me—if you think of me."

"You used me?" he repeated, his voice rough and gravelly. Angry and hurt. She couldn't bear to look at his face.

She blinked hard to hold back the tears. She wasn't going to cry in front of him and she didn't dare stick around to hear him tell her he didn't want anything more to do with her after today. "Goodbye, Eric," she said, and stumbled out into the corridor.

"Lola," he called after her, "stop. I'm not finished with you." She picked up speed. It had taken all her courage to come down here to apologize. She'd used it all up. She couldn't take any more. She heard footfalls. Bare feet on carpet, then what sounded like someone stumbling and a muffled curse. She kept on walking, almost running, as she hurried past the medical center toward the parallel corridor that led to the main dining room and the hotel lobby. Surely, he wouldn't follow her there into a public space in his bathrobe just to finish breaking her heart.

"LOLA, YOU ARE NOT sitting up here feeling sorry for yourself all evening when Antonio and I have made such lovely plans for dinner for all of us. I won't allow it." Myra sounded just as she had when Lola was ten and wallowing in self-pity over some imagined injury to her self-esteem.

Except she wasn't ten any longer, and this hurt was very, very real.

"I'll just make everyone this miserable if I go to the dining room with you," Lola said.

"Not if you put some effort into it."

"Mom, I just ruined what could have been something wonderful between Eric and me because I didn't play by the rules I've always set down for my life."

"How do you know it's ruined? It sounds to me like you didn't stick around long enough to get Eric's reaction, let alone come to the conclusion he never wants to see you again."

Lola stood up. She should have stayed in her cabin instead of coming up to her mother's suite to wallow in her misery in comfort and style, but Fran and Bonnie had fussed over her like two mother hens until she couldn't take it anymore. Fran had never once even hinted at "I told you so" over her failure to be completely honest and up front with Eric, and Bonnie hovered and consoled and vowed she never for a moment would have thought he was capable of letting Lola walk out of his life over nothing more than a misunderstanding. "I'm usually not that bad a judge of character, but this time I sure read the man wrong," she had said, shaking her head.

"All right. I give up," her mother was saying, throwing her hands in the air. The movement jerked Lola's attention back from the heartache that filled her entire body. "Go ahead. Feel sorry for yourself instead of going out there and hunting down Eric Lashman and setting everything right between you."

"I tried to do that, Mom," she said, suddenly tired of explaining, of reliving the humiliation of confronting him half naked in his cabin and seeing the shock and disillusion in his gray eyes. That was what hurt the most, she thought. Knowing she had failed to live up to his image of her. The woman he seemed to be falling in love with.

"At least, let me talk to him—"

"No!" Lola spun on her heel, the skirt of her emerald-green cocktail dress swirling just above her knees. The dress had been a welcome-back gift from Myra. Seventy-five percent off in the ship's boutique, Bonnie had confided. All because of a tiny tear in a seam that she'd mended herself with the sewing kit she always carried when traveling. Lola felt the tiniest tug of a smile as she recalled the pride in her sister's eyes as she showed off her handiwork.

"Oh, honey. Don't be so much like your father for once," Myra said, reaching out to take Lola's hands between her own.

"What do you mean?"

"He was a good man and I loved him. I still do love him. But you said it yourself, you always play by the rules. So did he. And what did it get him? Dead before he was old enough to start collecting social security. For once don't think that way. Start breaking the rules. At least a few of them."

"Like you are, Mom? Are you in love with Antonio?"

"In some ways, yes."

"Would you go to Spain to be with him?"

"I'd think about it. But I couldn't leave my grandchildren, all of you and move so far away for good." She smiled a little sadly. "You see, I'm too old to break all my own rules. But you're not."

"Maybe you could bend a few, Mom," Lola said, squeezing her mother's hands.

Myra laughed and threw her arms around Lola's neck, reaching up on tiptoe to give her a hug. "Oh, honey, I just might. I may not be able to live in Spain but I can surely visit, right?"

"Exactly." And, if her mother could spend part of her

life in Spain, Lola the homebody could spend part of her time in South Africa or Corsica or Dubai—or wherever else Eric was designing a golf course.

Myra stepped back, still smiling, and brushed a tear from the corner of her eye. "Oh, dear, if we keep this up I'm going to spoil my makeup. Now go, Lola. Make things right with Eric."

"What if he doesn't—" She was beginning to feel a tiny glimmer of hope deep inside her, faint and frail, but growing stronger with each beat of blood through her veins.

"Take the chance, Lola. If it's not meant to be then he'll tell you. But give him that chance. Grab happiness with both hands and hang on for dear life. Don't sit here and let it all slip away without trying to make it right. Don't live with regret for the next fifty years. For my sake, please, don't do that."

Lola gave her mother one last, quick hug. She would go find Eric and do as Myra asked. "If it works we'll join you for dessert—I can't miss the baked Alaska," she said, trying very hard not to sound as scared as she felt.

Myra nodded and shooed her toward the door. "I'll order an extra serving for Eric," she said in a tone that left no room for doubt. "Now go."

CHAPTER TWENTY-ONE

"MRS. SANDLER. LADIES. Good evening. Another beautiful night, isn't it?" He was in fine form tonight, Mike O'Connor thought, practically channeling old Spence. "Mendoza," he said, lifting one eyebrow as the Spaniard stood to welcome him to their table.

"Padre. Won't you join us for a glass of wine?"

"Why, thanks, old man, I'd love to, but like yourself, I'm dining with four lovely ladies. You understand, of course."

"Of course." Mendoza resumed his seat, moving his chair a few inches closer to the widow's just to show Mike who was top dog at this table. He got the hint and backed off a step or two.

"Speaking of lovely ladies, where is your youngest daughter, if I may ask?"

"She has an important engagement to see to before she joins us," Myra said serenely.

From the corner of his eye he saw the daughters exchange glances and smiles. *So, that was the way the wind was blowing with the golf pro, eh?*

"Well, if you will excuse me, I see my dinner guests coming into the dining room." One of the perks he liked best about this gig was the food. He had gained five pounds since he'd come on board. And tonight's entrée was Lobster Florentine. Even sharing the meal with Gloria Broadman couldn't spoil that treat. He'd taken to wearing the full Father Flanagan getup to dinner. The cassock was great for hiding that extra roll of fat. "If I don't get a chance to see you ladies again, have a safe voyage home."

He held out his hand to Myra once more. There was always the off chance she might still pony up a little something for "his boys."

"We've enjoyed your company, Father," she said, looking him straight in the eye. "I'll have my nephew— he's a tax accountant, you recall—see to my donation to 'your boys' when I return to Florida. I want to make sure all the *t*'s are crossed and the *i*'s dotted." She tilted her head, giving him a brilliant smile, but her eyes were are hard as the diamonds on her fingers. "It's so important to do these things right, don't you agree?"

"Of course." A warning chill slithered down his spine. Hopefully by the time her bean-counting nephew worked his way through the maze of phony addresses and nonexistent telephone numbers Mike'd set up and figured out St. Meinrad's School for Boys no longer existed, Mike'd be living the high life in the Caribbean.

"Padre," Mendoza asked, in that Castilian grandee accent of his, "has there been any word on the whereabouts of Miss Bennett? We have heard rumors that she never returned to the ship from her day trip to Naples. We are concerned for her."

Mike rested his hand over the cross on his chest and put on his most pious face, although his heart was racing a mile a minute. Another chill raised the short hairs on the back of his neck. They might already be discussing a dead woman. He'd talked to Tzekas a few moments before entering the dining room. They weren't the only people interested in having Ariana Bennett shadowed to the dig near Paestum, it seemed. Someone else had taken the trouble of siccing the *camorra,* the Naples mob, on her. And it didn't take a rocket scientist to figure out who that "someone" was. It was a turn of events Mike hadn't expected, and didn't bode well for the continued longevity of the ship's librarian. Or his and Tzekas's if they didn't keep their mouths shut and play along. The *camorra* played for keeps. He didn't intend to forget that salient fact, or he might be the next crew member to go missing.

"I'm sorry to say there's been no word from her," he said, drawing his thick white brows together in a look of concern. "But let us hope all is well and that her being left behind turns out as happily as the return of your daughter and Eric Lashman after their adventure on Corsica."

Once more the three Sandler women exchanged glances and smiles. Myra lifted her wineglass in a little toast. "Amen to that, Father."

IT WAS FULL DARK when the nameless one and the man named Nico came for her. She had been locked in the underground room, hidden from curious eyes by the rickety construction shed built on top of it. She was tired, hungry, thirsty and scared. The ship had sailed hours ago, she realized, but was anyone even aware she hadn't sailed with it?

She had regretted not telling someone where she was going the moment the dark, scarred man named Nico had confronted her after her arrival at the small, out-of-the-way dig near the archeological complex at Paestum. He hadn't even pretended to be part of the dig team—unlike the other menacing stranger who accompanied him each time he came to the shack to interrogate her.

She had done her best not to give them too much information about her father, but it was hard to keep silent when the threats had escalated with each visit. They had taken her purse, but she still had her iPod, with its precious information, in her skirt pocket. She closed her hand around it and wished it was a gun.

She had the terrible feeling that, when the two men who had been holding her prisoner came back again, they wouldn't come to talk. Not this time. It had been over twenty-four hours since she'd arrived at the site, with the guide Giorgio Tzekas had told her to hire if she was determined to go to Paestum, and who drove off as if all the devils in hell were after him the moment Niko and the other man had appeared from the ruins of the small Greek temple they were excavating.

That should have clued her in to run for her life, too. But she hadn't. Determined to help clear her father's name, no matter what the risk, she'd stood her ground. And soon found herself chained to a wall in a dark underground room, bullied and threatened and scared out of her wits.

Kidnapped. She still couldn't wrap her mind around the reality of it.

She heard the door of the shed open and close and heavy footfalls on the steps. She felt her muscles sag in relief. Until that moment, she had let herself believe they might never come back. Leaving her to die alone in the dark.

The light of the battery-operated lantern silhouetted one of her kidnappers, the nameless one. He was young, tall, with a full head of dark hair, features that might have come off one of the Greek and Roman coins found at the dig site, and eyes that were as cold and hard as agates.

Nico, the older man, had had no compunction at all about telling her his name. That fact alone made him even more frightening than his companion. If you kidnapped a woman, held her hostage for over twenty-four hours and didn't bother to keep your face or your name hidden, it could be for only one reason.

She was meant never to leave this room alive.

"Well, *signorina,*" Nico said in English, "it's time for you to leave us. You have given us all the information we need."

"You're letting me go?" Ariana asked before she could stop herself. If that happened it would be a miracle. And she didn't believe in miracles, anymore.

"Alas, no. I cannot let you go." The man showed yellow teeth in a feral grin. "I tire of your stubbornness. You are just too much trouble, bitch."

Fear rose like bile in her throat. She thought of her mother, the shock and the horror she'd feel when she learned Ariana was missing. When she learned she'd been murdered in cold blood. "Look. I won't press charges. I won't even notify the police. Just let me go." She turned to look at the nameless one. She was proud that she didn't sound like she was begging. She thought she caught a flicker of admiration in his obsidian eyes but he didn't speak, didn't even move a muscle.

Nico shook his head. "*Mi dispiace.* I'm sorry. That is not possible." He pulled a long, wicked-looking knife from his boot and started toward her. "Time to make your peace with God."

Ariana grabbed the chain that held her to the wall with both hands and jerked as hard as she could. It didn't budge. Pain shot up her arm and into her shoulders as Nico hauled her backward against him. "Don't try that again," he said, and she felt the cold blade of the knife against her throat. This was how she would die, alone with two monsters, her life's blood draining out on the hard ground that formed the floor of the underground room.

"Stop." The nameless one spoke for the first time. His voice was as big and hard as the rest of him. "You fool. If she's found with her throat cut, there will be hell to pay."

"Who says she will be found?" The pressure of the knife blade lessened a fraction of a degree. Nico shifted Ariana's body so that he could face the other man. "What do you suggest I do, genius?"

"I'll take care of her." He spoke in English so that she could understand. But she didn't understand. Her thoughts were starting to spiral off in terror and it took all her concentration to hold on to her reason, to hope she could find the means to escape, to live.

"A bullet hole will cause just as much trouble as a knife," Nico scoffed. "And more noise."

"I won't use a gun." He put his hand in the pocket of his jacket and produced a syringe. Ariana's knees went weak with fear, but she forced herself to remain upright. "Sit her in the chair and hold her still. But no bruises."

"Since when are you the one to give orders?" Nico snarled, but he began moving Ariana back toward the overturned chair. The nameless one hooked his foot around it, hauled it upright, and Nico pushed her down on the seat, one arm around her neck, one on the top of her head holding her down.

"Since you are making such a mess of it." He knelt before her. "I'm sorry," he said, "I have to do this. Don't be afraid, Little One."

Little One? The insult galvanized Ariana into one more effort to break free. Nico didn't hesitate. The arm around her throat tightened until she saw stars and colored moons spinning before her eyes. One muttered growl from the man on the floor and the deadly pressure eased, but not before she felt the sting of the needle on her skin.

"It will be painless," he said again, his voice curiously soothing. "You will fall asleep and it will be over."

Already the drug, the poison, was working. She could feel it weighing on her bones, dulling her senses. Her eyes fixed on his, dark and compelling—without a hint of mercy. "Don't fight. Sleep, Little One. It will be over soon."

She tried to fight but it was no use. Darkness crept over her. She was dying, she realized, and she'd failed in her quest. She'd failed to exonerate her father, give him back his good name and his reputation. *Oh, Daddy, I'm so sorry.* She blinked hard and focused once more on the compelling black eyes of her murderer. "I tried," she whispered. "I tried so hard." And then she knew no more.

LOLA FOUND HIM on the observation deck hitting biodegradeable golf balls out into the darkness of the sea. She stood quietly for a moment, watching the fluid play of muscles beneath his shirt, the seeming effortlessness of his upswing, the power of his downstroke as the clubhead sliced through the air and sent the ball spiraling off into space.

She glanced around the large open space, relieved to find it nearly deserted. The passengers who had dined on lobster and filet mignon and baked Alaska at the first seating were in the theater watching the show, or dancing in the nightclubs or changing out of their formal wear into more comfortable clothes to party long into the night in the ship's discos and bars. They wouldn't migrate to the observation deck until later, when the last of the sunset had faded from rose to violet to charcoal in the western sky and the stars had come into their own.

Those who dined at the late seating, like her mother and sisters, were just finding their way into the dining room after cocktails and hors d'oeurves and sitting for portraits in their formal wear. Eric was dressed formally, too, or at least he had been. His tux jacket was draped over his bag of clubs, his shirt sleeves were rolled to just below his elbows and his tie was undone. He was all male, all athlete and breathtaking.

If all goes well, we'll join you for dessert.

She gathered her courage and took a step toward him, catching his attention when she moved out of the shadow of the companionway. Eric straightened, then leaned one hand on the head of his club, crossing his legs as he watched her approach.

"I was hoping I'd find you here," she said, straining to get the words past the constriction in her throat. Her hands were so tightly linked she could feel the bones of her knuckles grind together. She tried to relax.

"I was told, in no uncertain terms, to wait here until you showed up," he said cryptically.

"What?"

"Your mother," he replied without anger but with no trace of warmth in his voice, either.

Lola's stomach rolled but she kept on walking toward him. "You've talked to my mother?" Why was she surprised? Myra had said she was going to start breaking some of her own rules, one of which had been never to involve herself in her daughters' love lives.

"Yes," he said, "she called my cabin and told me to get myself up here." He twirled the club through his fingers and back again as though it were no bigger than a soda straw. "She ordered me not to budge until you got here. Under no circumstances was I to show my face in the dining room until we had talked."

"I should have known," Lola said, but the roiling sickness in her stomach had been replaced by the tickling flight of butterflies.

He twirled the club through his fingers once more and set it down between his feet, leaning on it like the handle of a cane. "Why did you run away from me this afternoon?"

"I'd said everything I came to your cabin to say," she replied, coming closer, leaning her hip against the teak railing so that she had something firm against her back. Her knees were trembling and so were her hands. He wasn't laughing, wasn't even smiling, but she could see a glint of something close to amusement in his normally unreadable gray eyes.

"Why didn't you stop when I asked you to?"

"I didn't hear you," she said. It was only half a lie. But even that was too much. "I...I was afraid you only wanted to tell me to go to hell. That you never wanted to see me again."

"I bloody well nearly broke my neck tripping over the bulkhead coming after you," he said, leaning forward with a delicious hint of menace in his stance. "Lost my towel, too, and I wasn't alone in the corridor," he added darkly.

She tried not to picture the scene for fear she would break out in nervous giggles. "I'm sorry— You came after me? Why?"

"Why? Because I didn't want our first fight to be our last one, that's why." He slid the club back into the bag with the same aplomb as a knight sliding his sword back into its scabbard. He reached out and took her by the shoulders. His hands were big and strong, and her breath caught on a little sob because , just minutes ago, she'd thought she'd never feel their warmth on her skin again.

"Why did you lie to me about your job, Lola?"

"I explained all that," she said.

"It wasn't that coherent," he replied, the faintest hint of a smile curving the corners of his mouth.

"I feel like enough of a fool. Don't make me go through it again, just know that I'm so very sorry I wasn't totally honest with you from the start."

"It hurts a bloke's ego to find out you weren't just bowled over by his charms from the get-go, you know?"

"Will it make you feel better if I tell you the bowled-over part came about forty-eight hours later?"

"Not my personal best," he said, "but it will serve." He pulled her close and she let him, resting her palms on his chest to keep a little distance between them.

"And why did you chase after me in your bathrobe, if I'm just another one of your conquests?" she asked in her turn.

"Competitive nature," he said, nuzzling her neck.

Lola lifted her head and stared at the stars, but she didn't see anything for the fireworks going off in her head. Their kiss was long and slow and filled with promises given and taken.

"A week ago I didn't even know you," he said, and she was pleased to hear him breathless.

"And tonight?"

"Tonight I want to spend with you. Tonight and every night for the rest of my life."

"I love you, Eric," she said, suddenly filled with courage and hope. "I'll try never to hurt you again."

"I love you, Lola," he said. He brushed his hands across her hair. "But don't make promises you can't keep. It will only make you unhappy. Life is a hard lie sometimes. Don't make it worse by expecting perfection from yourself. Or from me. Let's just do our best. We'll argue and bicker and fight just like every other married couple, but we'll always make up because we love each other."

"Married couple," she whispered. "I like the sound of that. Say that again." She wrapped her arms around his neck.

"Marry me, Lola. Marry me. Have my children, come with me to the ends of the earth."

"Yes," she said. "Yes, to all those things."

"Even to the-ends-of-the-earth part?"

"Yes."

"Will you let me teach you to play golf? For our children's sake. So we can play as a family."

"You drive a hard bargain. But for our children's sake, yes, again."

"What about your job?"

"That's all it is. A job. You're my job now." She smiled as his dark brows pulled together in a slight frown. "And as for a career, I can find a new one. One that's worthy of my talents—whatever they turn out to be. If you'll stand by me."

"It's a deal."

She was breaking all her own rules and she didn't care. Suddenly, in Eric's arms, anything seemed possible. New careers, traveling halfway around the world and then back again, children with dual citizenships.

"When we have children," she said, nibbling his lower lip, feeling him grow hard against her softness, wanting him and needing him, "I want them to be born in the States. Our daughter might want to be president one day."

"I think I can agree to that. As a matter of fact, if you kiss me again, I think I'd agree to just about anything."

She obliged. When his mouth left hers and she'd caught her breath again, she raised her hands to frame his face. "I love you," she said again. "And now it's time to go down to the dining room. We don't want to miss the baked Alaska."

* * * * *

MEDITERRANEAN NIGHTS
*Join the glamorous world of cruising
with the guests and crew of*
Alexandra's Dream—*the newest luxury ship to
set sail on the romantic Mediterranean.
The voyage continues in October 2007 with*
AN AFFAIR TO REMEMBER
by Karen Kendall

The daughter of a shipping tycoon, Helena Stamos
has led a privileged life, but, for the past fifteen years,
that life has also been filled with heartache—ever
since Nikolas Pappas left her without a word.
Back then a mere deckhand, Nikolas is suddenly back
in her life as captain of her father's cruise ship,
Alexandra's Dream. But, even if they can see beyond
their past, what's to stop Nick from leaving
Helena…again?

Here's a preview!

NOW HE STOOD IN THE moonlight again with the boss's daughter. He was a captain now, not a deckhand, but it made no difference. All of the shiny buttons on his dress uniform were nothing but brass.

They didn't hold a candle to the flawless emeralds in her ears or anything else in her jewelry box. Top brass had nothing on royalty and, to Nick, Helena was royalty.

He'd never confronted her about what he'd learned, which was unlike him. He'd simply been too stunned. He'd made love to her one last time in the little bed, pretending that everything was fine.

"Is something bothering you, Nikolas?" she had asked.

"No, *agape mou*," he'd lied. Because he still hadn't made up his mind to walk away. He hadn't bought an engagement ring lightly.

But in the small hours of the morning, as he'd watched her sleep, he'd, at last, come reluctantly to a decision. Even if she wasn't playing him, slumming for fun, he couldn't marry someone who'd deliberately hidden her identity from him. And the daughter of Elias Stamos, a billionaire, wouldn't have him, anyway. It was out of the question.

He could have woken her. Could have gotten some kind of explanation. Could have said goodbye. But, instead, he'd moved silently around the tiny room, gathering his things into his ancient duffel bag. She hadn't stirred once.

He'd stood gazing at her; almost changed his mind. Then he'd bent and kissed her lightly on the lips before leaving for good.

So what was he doing with her in his arms tonight? Torturing himself? Trying to relive the past?

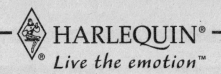

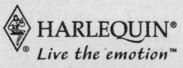

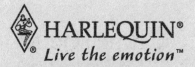

HARLEQUIN®
INTRIGUE®

BREATHTAKING ROMANTIC SUSPENSE

Shared dangers and passions lead to electrifying
romance and heart-stopping suspense!

Every month, you'll meet six new heroes
who are guaranteed to make your spine tingle
and your pulse pound. With them you'll enter
into the exciting world of Harlequin Intrigue—
where your life is on the line
and so is your heart!

THAT'S INTRIGUE—
ROMANTIC SUSPENSE
AT ITS BEST!

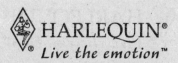

HARLEQUIN®
Live the emotion™

HARLEQUIN®

Super Romance®

...there's more to the story!

Superromance.
A *big* satisfying read about unforgettable
characters. Each month we offer *six* very different
stories that range from family drama to adventure
and mystery, from highly emotional stories to
romantic comedies—and much more! Stories
about people you'll believe in and care about.
Stories too compelling to put down....

Our authors are among today's *best* romance
writers. You'll find familiar names and talented
newcomers. Many of them are award winners—
and you'll see why!

If you want the biggest and best
in romance fiction, you'll get it
from Superromance!

Exciting, Emotional, Unexpected...

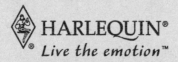

HARLEQUIN®
Live the emotion™

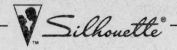

SPECIAL EDITION™

Emotional, compelling stories that capture the intensity of living, loving and creating a family in today's world.

Modern, passionate reads that are powerful and provocative.

Dramatic and sensual tales of paranormal romance.

Silhouette® Romantic SUSPENSE

Romances that are sparked by danger and fueled by passion.